"Am I making myself clear, Christa?"

She blinked, dragging her unseeing gaze away from her barely tasted wine, meeting Ross's unfathomable eyes.

"In exchange for discharging your father's debt I would take this house, and in return I would guarantee to restore it, to allow him to live here for his lifetime if he wishes to do so, to provide him with an occupation compatible with his standing."

"You still haven't told me how much Father owes."

"I believe that's for him to tell you, not me," he replied, moving closer, watching her face. "But I do have one more condition to make."

"Fire away," she said, knowing it wouldn't affect the outcome of her decision.

"The other condition is that you agree to become my wife."

DIANA HAMILTON creates high-tension conflict that brings new life to traditional romance. Readers find her a welcome addition to Harlequin and look forward to new novels by this talented author.

Books by Diana Hamilton

Don't miss any of our special offers. Write to us at the following address for information on our newest releases.

Harlequin Reader Service
P.O. Box 1397, Buffalo, NY 14240
Canadian address: P.O. Box 603,
Fort Erie, Ont. L2A 5X3

DIANA HAMILTON

an inconvenient marriage

Harlequin Books

TORONTO • NEW YORK • LONDON
AMSTERDAM • PARIS • SYDNEY • HAMBURG
STOCKHOLM • ATHENS • TOKYO • MILAN
MADRID • WARSAW • BUDAPEST • AUCKLAND

Harlequin Presents first edition April 1992
ISBN 0-373-11449-4

Original hardcover edition published in 1990
by Mills & Boon Limited

AN INCONVENIENT MARRIAGE

CHAPTER ONE

THE tall stranger walked purposefully towards the big house, his feet crunching decisively on the weed-spattered drive.

Christa slammed to a halt on the stone steps leading down from the main door, her heart beginning to thump. Few people called at Liddiat Hall nowadays, and certainly not at just gone six in the morning.

Unable to control the tremor of nerves that made her fingers shake, she tightened the belt of the robe she'd flung on, making her waist look impossibly tiny, and made a conscious effort to stiffen her shoulders.

Hearing a car arrive, she had thought it must be Father and had come racing downstairs, reprimands and anxious questions bubbling with equal intensity on the tip of her tongue. Since she had come back to live here she had discovered that he often stayed out late. But he had never stayed out all night before.

So was it bad news? She couldn't imagine why a stranger should be calling at this hour unless it was to break the news of an accident.

He looked sombre enough, she noted apprehensively as the stranger drew nearer—the uncompromisingly male features beneath the dark thatch of hair were cast in grim lines, the wide mouth harsh.

Pushing trembling fingers through long, rumpled silver-gilt hair, she eyed him warily, flutters of terrible apprehension beating sickeningly through her veins, her violet eyes enormous, dwarfing a small classical nose, a curving rosebud mouth, a stubborn chin.

At close quarters he looked intimidating, his body packed with power—lithe and whippy, a veritable dynamo of a man, a man who made her feel threatened, out of her depth. A stupid reaction, surely, and engendered by her apprehension, the blessed voice of inner reason reminded her as he asked, 'Christa Liddiat?' The deep smooth voice was slightly mocking, as if he knew perfectly well who she was and wasn't bowled over by it.

As he held out a hand—long-fingered, strong—the early morning June sunlight drew muted glitters from the gold casing of the wafer-slim watch he wore on his wrist and a pearly sheen from square, perfectly manicured nails.

Her heart hammering, Christa pushed the tip of a pointed, cat-like tongue over her parted dry lips and muttered huskily, 'My father...?' Childishly, motivated by something she couldn't understand, she pushed her hands behind her back, ignoring his. 'Is he—is he all right?'

'He's fine, as far as I know.' Again the disquieting hint of mockery, lying just beneath the surface. 'I left him about an hour ago. In fact, he should be here at any moment. He suggested I came on ahead.'

He rocked back on his heels, his hands now thrust negligently into the pockets of neatly fitting dark narrow trousers; his dinner-jacket was unbuttoned, pushed open to reveal the white pleated lawn of his shirt. 'He has a small—shall we say, business matter to sort out.'

At least nothing awful had happened to her father and she had to be thankful for that. But she still didn't know what this man was doing here, at this time of the morning, dressed in formal evening gear.

'Ross Donahue,' he introduced himself with mocking simplicity, his sensual male mouth quirking as if with some deep inner amusement. And again the extended hand. Violet eyes flicked up to meet inscrutable silver and she stifled a gasp as something dark and nameless jolted deep inside her. He didn't look as if he'd spent the night drinking and gambling with her father—just very sure of himself and stone cold sober.

This time there was no apprehension to excuse a lack of basic courtesy and, with a small resigned sigh, she gave him her hand, intending only a cool minimal touch. But he grasped her slender fingers and for some unknown reason the purpose in that tensile warmth had the power to shock her, making hot colour run along her cheekbones.

'I have been invited to spend the weekend here, as your father's guest,' he stated silkily, his fingers tightening over hers. Silver eyes mocked her coolly, almost as if inviting her disbelief, even as the unwelcome touch of his hand seared her skin.

Outraged, Christa jerked away from him, stalking back towards the main door. What did he take her for? A complete fool?

She didn't know him from Adam and, on his own admission, he'd left her father around an hour ago— which meant they'd spent at least the latter part of the night together at some club in town. And more than likely her father would have had too much to drink and lost more at the tables than he could afford to. And the combination would have made him indiscreet, vulnerable. So this opportunist joker would have decided to come on ahead, see what the pickings were, con his way into the house to see what he could walk away with.

Liddiat Hall was a good address—what this creep couldn't know was that there was nothing of any value left in it!

But for all her speed she wasn't quick enough and his presence, right behind her, almost made her panic.

'Please leave,' she commanded, summoning all the hauteur she was capable of, her Liddiat genes coming to her aid. 'I don't invite strangers with no credentials into my home.'

'Very sensible,' he stated drily, and she thought she saw a flicker of distaste ruffle the cool silver surface of his eyes as he registered the most imperious stare she was able to produce. Then he continued silkily, 'However, I have introduced myself and explained my reason for being here.'

'We don't entertain,' she informed him stonily, trying to ignore the panicky fear that picked up the speed of her pulse-beats. 'And I rather think my father would have told me had he decided to make an exception. And do you,' she tacked on, tartly cutting, 'make a habit of arriving at six in the morning? You must be a wow with your hosts!'

Her sarcasm, instead of shaming him, or serving to let him know he wasn't dealing with a gullible fool, only seemed to amuse him.

'Would you believe me if I told you that for the first time ever I have allowed impatience to overcome my normally strict observance of protocol?' Humour darkened his eyes, curled his mouth into a smile that made her understand how easily some women could be conned by some men. But not this woman. Not this man.

She said baldly, anger with his dangerous urbanity making her forget her very real fear. 'I'm afraid not. I do believe, however, that you are a dirty opportunist. And I suggest you cut your losses and walk out now.'

For a moment he was still, very still, his eyes narrowing above hard, jutting cheekbones, his mouth tight with an anger she could almost reach out and touch. She was afraid, more afraid than if he'd used violence, and she dragged in a breath and blustered, 'If you don't leave, this minute, I'll call my father's staff to throw you out.'

'Your father has no "staff".' He called her bluff, his eyes lethal. 'The last employee was dismissed over six months ago.'

Christa went cold, her footsteps faltering on the scuffed oak-block flooring. Last Christmas she had very reluctantly given up her high-powered secretarial job and had come home, finding herself work in the small local market town, determined to make her father see sense.

But far from persuading him to sell Liddiat Hall—a great barn of a place which it was impossible to keep comfortable, let alone clean, without plentiful paid help—she had found herself parting with her entire savings. Mrs Perkins, who had been housekeeper here for as long as Christa could remember, had been the only employee left at that time, and she hadn't been paid for almost nine months. Handing over her own hard-earned savings as back pay, plus a glowing reference, Christa had had to let her go.

But how did this Donahue creature—if that was his real name, which she distinctly doubted—know that?

'The police, then!' she snapped, her backbone stiffening. She would not show fear in front of anyone, least of all him!

'That would be most unwise,' Donahue drawled, close enough for his breath to set tendrils of silvery curls brushing lovingly against her cheek.

Startled by the horrible intimacy, she shied away from him, then turned to face him when she judged she had covered a safe distance.

'Unwise for whom? For you, I should imagine!'

He shook his head in rebuttal, setting free one dark lock of hair to lie like a comma above slanting brows.

'Embarrassing for your father.'

She didn't believe that, not for one moment, and whatever his true reasons for being here she just *knew* they couldn't be good.

Finding herself suddenly at a loss for words, her eyes sped wildly over the huge hall, the dreadful shabbiness cruelly intensified by the early morning sunlight which streamed in through the open main door. Motes of dust danced in the golden rays, settling on the dull oak parquet, on table-tops denuded of any ornaments worth more than a few pounds, drifting upwards to gather in the cobwebs on the high rafters.

From the corners of her eyes she noted that he was giving the surroundings a much closer scrutiny than her own, his eyes narrowed assessingly.

So maybe this—this trickster—was already deciding he was wasting his time. Oh, how she hoped so! He had admitted to knowing that her father could no longer afford to employ the help needed to keep the huge house and gardens as they should be, and now the evidence of his own eyes would surely be telling his intelligent yet no doubt twisted brain that there were no pickings left here worth the having.

She groaned inwardly, her eyes unable to avoid the lighter oblong patches on the walls where family portraits had once hung. She and her father might be down on their uppers, but they were Liddiats still, and the fighting blood of the ancestor who had won this land, and far more besides, in the time of Henry the Seventh, coupled with that of the many others in her family who had hung on to it ever since, began coursing hotly through her veins.

So she was able to turn and face him, her head held high, every aristocratic line of her greyhound slenderness rigid with the grim determination to rid herself of his strangely dangerous and definitely unwelcome presence as she intoned icily, 'As you can no doubt see, there's nothing here for you.'

'You think not?' he countered, coolly suave. 'There, I'm afraid, you are very, very wrong.' A small smile hovered around the corners of his undeniably attractive mouth, but his eyes held a strangely compelling, watchful quality which disturbed her more than she cared to admit. It was as if he were weighing her up, imprinting every aspect of her appearance on his mind, reading her soul. His impertinence appalled her, his lack of reaction to her pointedly imperative words unnerving her.

Suddenly, he gave her the doubtful benefit of his heart-jolting smile and Christa's mouth went dry. She swallowed convulsively. Fear, she told herself staunchly, fear of what he might do when he discovered that his conning activities had been a total waste of time, and that she, a vulnerable female, here alone, was the only witness to his dishonest attempts. It was fear—nothing whatever to do with the way that smile changed his face, flooding the beautifully sculpted, remote features with warmth, the silver eyes crinkling at the corners, making them brim over with what she could only translate as sexual invitation, appreciation, making her horribly aware that the robe she had so hastily flung on was flimsy, to say the least.

Worriedly, she slicked her tongue over the sudden dryness of her full lips and then found herself trembling as his wicked eyes focused deliberately on her mouth, on the small, betraying movement of her tongue.

Immediately, shamingly, a wild heat burgeoned in the pit of her stomach, weakening her, spreading its insidious fire through her veins, and his smile faded, leaving his face tight, as if he recognised the subversive warmth that lapped her body—as if he felt it, too.

'Christa...' He stepped forward, his features softening, his eyes sober, as if he were about to say something of importance, and before she could react to the sheer gall of the rogue she visibly sagged with relief as she caught the sound of her father's dilapidated car coughing its way erratically along the drive.

She hurried to the open door, her movements jerky, more than half expecting him to try to stop her. But he did no such thing and she saw, when she compulsively turned her head, that he was standing exactly where he'd been before, hands in his pockets, his very ease a contemptuous thing in itself.

Watching her father tiredly getting out of the car, her heart sank. What hope had he of ridding their home of the stranger who was now in possession of the hall, acting almost as if he owned the place and had rights, when all her own attempts had failed?

Christa loved her father deeply, warts and all, but love didn't blind her to his manifest faults or prevent a sharp prick of irritation as she noted the way defeat was written into every sagging line of his face, the way he couldn't meet her eyes.

Since her mother's death ten years ago, when Christa herself had been only twelve, she had grown used to her father's mood swings, had understood that they sprang from the inability to come to terms with the untimely death of the wife he had adored, and had never ceased to adore and mourn in all the time that had passed.

But during the past twelve months his moods had grown progressively worse, which was why she had reluctantly put her own career into cold storage six months ago and had returned home to try to sort things out.

Not that she seemed to be having much success so far, she thought drily, noting with a twinge of compassion the way he seemed to have shrunk. The outdated, much cleaned dinner-jacket swamped him, the strand of grey hair he usually wore brushed jauntily across his bald head now fell limply to one side of his face, making him look pathetic.

He advanced towards her, his feet dragging, no doubt expecting the cutting edge of her tongue—a natural reaction to the way he'd stayed out all night, worrying her.

But right now that would have to wait. She needed him to keep an eye on the intruder—if he wasn't already ransacking the house—while she phoned the police. Not that she wanted that sort of trouble, but it was clear that nothing short of the strong arm of the law would persuade that suave so-and-so to leave!

She sped down the crumbling stone steps, feeling the summer breeze push against her face and lift her hair, agitated almost unbearably by the way he was deliberately taking his time. Heaven only knew what that smooth-tongued reprobate was up to now! And she was about to explain what had happened, what she wanted him to do, when her father shocked the tumbling words out of her brain.

'Is Donahue here? His car's further down the drive. You haven't been——' He bit back whatever he'd been about to say and gave her a curious look, almost furtive, before tacking on, studiously hearty, 'I hope you've shown him to a room, given him a good breakfast? I was delayed longer than I'd anticipated.' He pushed a shaky hand over his head, stroking back the errant strand, consciously straightening his shoulders.

Christa, feeling ridiculous, not to mention annoyed, uttered thickly, 'So you really did invite him to stay?'

'Of course. I expect he explained that much.' Again the vaguely furtive look, a faint flush of something—embarrassment?

Now that the immediate panic was over, Christa stood her ground, blocking his way as he attempted to move past her into the house. There were things she needed to say to him, to get clear, without that—that creature—listening to every word, taking cool amusement from her discomfiture.

'I think you might have warned me, or had the sense to arrive before him. And since when have you had weekend guests?' she derided, keeping her voice low because, for all she knew, that smooth devil was probably straining every auditory nerve-end to hear what she was saying. 'The house isn't exactly...' She spread her hands, words failing because words weren't really necessary. Her father knew the state of the place, the general dilapidation, the bathrooms that might have been a joke if they hadn't been so damned uncomfortable!

'I didn't have the opportunity,' Ambrose Liddiat defended pompously, puffing out his cheeks, using his rarely seen—and usually amusing—act of parental bluster, annoying Christa now into pricking that particular little bubble.

She countered sweetly, 'Then you only have yourself to blame. You should have made the opportunity because, I'm afraid, I tried to show your house guest the door, threatened him with the police.'

She smiled, her curvy lips hinting at the small degree of satisfaction she'd obtained as his mouth dropped open and he said, sounding strangled, 'You did *what*?'

'What can you expect? You chose to stay out all night, without bothering to phone and let me know not to expect you—then a total stranger arrives on the doorstep, at six o'clock on a Friday morning, announcing he's come for the weekend! What did you expect my reaction to be, for goodness' sake? I thought he was——'

'What you thought doesn't signify, my girl.' Her father's face was ashen, his voice low as he pushed past her. 'I spent the latter part of the night doing business with Donahue—this weekend was set up to finalise the deal.' He shot her a fleeting hunted look, muttering over his shoulder, 'I just pray to God you haven't ruined everything!'

Ruined what? Christa silently fumed, irritation lifting her stubborn chin a fraction as her stormy eyes watched her father's now rapid progress into the house. Whatever ruin he faced, he only had himself to blame.

A year ago she had discovered that he had started drinking more than was good for him, gambling with money he couldn't afford to lose. And six months after that she had known she had no option but to return home, to try to make him see sense, to persuade him to sell the family home and start his life again.

But so far he had refused to listen, informing her— when his volatile moods were having an upswing—that his gambling was a means of restoring the family fortunes.

And what was this so-called business deal he was supposed to be cooking up with Donahue? she fumed disgustedly. He had about as much business acumen as a bat—that was one of the reasons he was always in a financial mess!

No, she thought more soberly, he had obviously spent part of last night gambling with Donahue. So how much had he lost? And had Donahue, with his clever brain, his assessing silver eyes, decided that their home held enough of value to cover the debt?

Sometimes she despaired. She didn't think her father would ever learn that any form of gambling was a mug's game, with no certain winners, only losers.

Tightening her mouth, she mounted the steps and came face to face with Donahue on his way out.

'Leaving already?' She could no more have stopped the acidly sweet words from tripping off her tongue than she could have stopped her heart from beating. If she was right in her assumption—and everything pointed to it—then this suave devil had fastened on to her father's weakness last night and stripped him of lord only knew how much. And if he thought she was about to apologise for having accused him of being an opportunist thief, then he would have to think again because in her book that was exactly what he was!

'Sorry to disappoint you.' His beautifully structured face was deadpan but from the devilish glow of amusement in the black-fringed silver eyes Christa knew he was laughing at her and her cheeks flooded with furious colour as he explained lightly, 'I dropped in at my apartment on my way here—after Ambrose had extended his generous invitation—to pack a bag. I'm merely on my way to collect it from the car.'

A ghost of a smile, a slight raising of one blackly arched brow told Christa that, in his opinion, he had won that round, and she swung past him, into the house, anger darkening her eyes.

She ignored her father, who was hovering, and made for the stairs, but he caught her arm, swinging her round, his eyes anxious.

'Christa, you've every right to be annoyed with me—I'll give you that. But don't take it out on Ross. Be nice to him, for God's sake! He's done nothing wrong.'

'Hasn't he, Father?' Christa smiled tightly, extricating herself from his grasp. 'Forgive me if I prefer to reserve judgement.'

In the light of the fact of her father's invitation, then no, Ross Donahue hadn't done or said a thing out of place. Yet every instinct told her he was dangerous, a man to steer well clear of, a cool predator, a man who would take what he wanted with no questions asked, no apologies, a man who would walk through anyone who got in his way—wearing that uniquely devastating smile of his!

CHAPTER TWO

At HALF-PAST eight Christa was in the high street of the neighbouring small market town unlocking the door of the Rainbow Boutique.

She had had no qualms about leaving her father to deal as best he could with his house guest, none at all. If he wanted to invite every reprobate he met at his club then let him have the chore of finding a bedroom which didn't have a leaking ceiling, a broken window-pane or rotting floorboards. Let him allocate bedlinen and towels, make breakfast. She, Christa, had made it plain that she was doing none of those things.

She was feeling edgy and apprehensive, anxious about that so-called business deal—a euphemism for gambling debts if she'd ever heard one! And today was Friday, the only day of the week when she and Tania Clarke, who owned the boutique, worked together, and, much as she liked her friend, she could have done without too much company today.

Tania designed most of the garments on sale and spent four days a week in her studio or in the workrooms where half a dozen women were kept busy making up her designs. Only on the remaining two days did she visit the shop, on Fridays to go over the stock and the books, on Saturdays to keep in touch with the buying public and allow Christa the weekend off.

She was tidying the racks and shelves, prior to the day's trading, when Tania let herself in. Her dramatic outfit of a swirling scarlet cotton skirt and black peasant blouse, her tumbling mane of auburn hair, made a startling contrast with Christa's paler, more sophisticated beauty in the understated sleeveless charcoal linen shift she had chosen to wear today.

'Super weather!' Tania greeted her. 'We should move some of those beach outfits today. Love the way you've displayed them in the window, darling! Any coffee on?'

'It's just about ready.' Christa jerked her head towards the tiny kitchenette cum office at the rear end of the shop, dredging up a smile. Tania was a great girl, they had been firm friends since Pony Club days, but her exuberant personality was going to be difficult to take today, after a sleepless night worrying about her father's whereabouts followed by the totally unpleasant encounter with Ross Donahue at six this morning.

The morning went as predicted, the hot weather bringing a rush for cool cottons and beachwear. During her short lunch break Christa shopped sulkily for the weekend foodstuffs, her clothes sticking to her in the heat, the residue of anger and apprehension refusing to go away.

She didn't trust Ross Donahue, not an inch, and her father's follies were getting worse, as far as she could see. She wondered hopelessly what was happening right now, between the two of them, back at Liddiat Hall.

One thing was sure. She was going to have to give her father an ultimatum. If he had been gambling again last night, and she was fairly certain that was the case, then it had to be the last time. No falling from grace again, no more 'last flutters—quite harmless, m'dear!' Otherwise she would leave, take up her career again, and allow her father to go ahead and ruin himself in his own way.

Her thoughts were grim, her violet eyes even grimmer, as she stowed her purchases neatly in the office, bending to put the fresh minced beef she'd bought for this evening's lasagne in the minute fridge.

Tania, coming through from the front of the premises, said, 'What's up, darling? You've been looking like a wet weekend all day.'

'Have I? I'm sorry.' Christa stood up slowly. 'Nothing's wrong,' she lied.

'Pull the other one.' Tania draped herself across the top of the desk, her scarlet skirts spreading out around long tanned legs. 'Tell auntie all. What are friends for, anyway? Man trouble?'

If only it were that simple. The only trouble Christa had had with her men friends had been cooling the relationship if they had shown signs of becoming too serious or too amorous. So far she had been too interested in furthering her career, maintaining her independence, to make time for any serious commitment.

Christa shook her head, her smile wry, 'No such luck! It's Father, I'm afraid.'

'Up to his old tricks?'

Christa nodded, her eyes bleak. There was little point in pretending. The old county families, almost without exception, stuck together, knew everything that was worth knowing, and a lot that wasn't, about each other. It had been Tania's mother who had written to her in the first place, gently advising her to try to do something about Ambrose Liddiat's newly emerging gambling habits.

But she wasn't prepared to mention Ross Donahue or the business deal that Christa just knew had more to do with gambling debts. The danger she intuitively sensed in that tall dark predator, the man with the cool assessing silver eyes, was too immediate, too stark to put into words, too frightening in a way she couldn't fully define.

'If I were you, I'd leave him to stew,' Tania advised bluntly. 'You've done all you can, heaven knows. And although I'd miss you around here like hell, you should get back to your career. You were in line for promotion, weren't you?'

'It had been mooted.' Christa put the kettle on for a much needed cup of tea. The early afternoon was usually slack and she needed something to make her feel less jaded. 'And my old job's open for me, when I can go back.'

A sharp pang of regret pierced her, regret for the life she'd made for herself before she'd felt she had to come home to try to stop her father from wrecking his life.

She'd been secretary to the manager of a high-flying London advertising agency, had taken weekend and night courses in management, accountancy and, latterly, commercial design, hardly spending any time at all in the small flat she had shared with another girl from the same company, just crashing into bed at the end of each long day of hard work and study.

But it had paid off in the end because her boss had given her very strong hints that the position of his PA would be open to her when the present incumbent, Martin Brand, was moved on to the board.

'Go back now, you're wasting your talents here—when I offered you this job I honestly thought it would merely be a stopgap for a few weeks until you got old Ambrose sorted out. The money I pay you has got to be peanuts compared with the salary you were earning before. And much as I like your father—who doesn't?—you can't waste your life simply because he refuses to listen to reason.'

Which was all perfectly true, and very logical, Christa acknowledged inwardly as she poured boiling water into the teapot. But logic had little to do with loving and caring, and, despite her earlier grim intention to leave him to sort out his own messes unless he stopped gambling and agreed to sell up and start afresh, she knew she couldn't do it. She said huskily, 'It's a form of sickness, Tania. He can't help himself, so I have to try to help him; there's no one else. He was forty years old when I was born, fifty-two when mother died ten years ago—and he's never really got over the loss. He loved her so very much. But even so, even in those early days, he always put me first. He made sure I never felt deprived—he shared so much with me, he went out of his way to do so. He shouldered both parental roles and performed them to the best of his ability, and that's why,' she stated with simple conviction, 'I just can't walk out on him and leave him to wreck his life.'

Ambrose came into the kitchen as she was unpacking the groceries. The house had felt deserted as she'd entered and if she hadn't seen Donahue's black Lotus Elan on the driveway she could have believed herself to be alone.

'You look tired, poppet. A hard day?'

She wanted to say no, a hard night, worrying because you didn't come home. But she bit her tongue on that one. Something was brewing, she could sense it in the way he was so twitchy, his hands shaking as he took over the unpacking, stowing the last of the groceries away for her.

'What precisely is this business deal you're cooking up with Donahue?' she asked bluntly, in no mood for evasion because she didn't think that 'business deal' were the right words to use to describe what was going on around here.

But evasion was what she got, pure and simple, as he told her gruffly, 'I think the whole thing would be better coming from him.' He avoided her eyes. 'He's in a position to help us considerably, put it that way. With a little co-operation on our parts, we could see Liddiat Hall put in order again, never have a moment's financial worry again. What do you say to that, eh? Now off you go,' He gave her a little shove, doing his best to smile. 'I know he's anxious to talk the whole thing over with you, so go and change into something pretty, and for heaven's sake, child, be nice to the man, listen to what he has to say. He's in a position to make or break us, just bear that in mind.'

'Tell me what it's all about!' Christa dug her heels in, her head spinning. Make or break? Donahue? Never a moment's financial worry? It sounded an incredible scenario, she couldn't believe a word of it.

What possible reason could Donahue have for expending the serious money needed to restore the Hall, and to ensure that her father never suffered a moment's financial worry again? Ambrose didn't have an asset in the world apart from a couple of acres of Hertfordshire land and a crumbling old house which, in Christa's honest opinion, would be better sold off for what it would fetch.

So what did her father have to put into this airy-fairy business deal? What did he have that Ross Donahue could possibly want? It simply didn't make sense!

'I'd rather you heard it from him, and so would he.' He sounded stubborn as a mule, but his eyes were misty and Christa gave an exasperated snort and decided that she'd have to get it from the horse's mouth, much as she disliked the idea.

'Be nice to the man.' The words rang heavily in her ears. Her father had said that, twice, and he'd sounded as if he meant every word. But why should she? How could she, when every instinct told her to distrust him, when each time she'd faced him her overwhelming impression had been one of danger?

And as for changing into something pretty, she'd be damned if she would! He could take her as he found her. And she walked down the stairs after bathing away the stickiness of the day wearing a clean but ancient black T-shirt and a pair of light cotton jeans.

And he was waiting for her in the hall, sprawled out in one of the shabby armchairs that faced the huge empty stone fireplace.

He got to his feet when he heard her, sheer animal grace explicit in every indolent movement, relaxed as a cat, and she felt again the inexplicable tremor of alerted nerve-ends, the sudden acceleration of her pulse-beats.

She had never, ever, been so aware of a man, of the undeniable signals her senses were receiving. They added up to one thing, and one thing only: beware, be wary. And so she was.

'You have something to say to me?' Her voice was tight, her smile nothing more than a frozen muscle contraction, not reaching her eyes, barely moving her lips.

'I have.' His own smile was warm, but it didn't touch his eyes, either. They narrowed to enquiring slits of pewter, holding a question she couldn't fathom, didn't want to.

But at least he would give answers to the questions her father had side-stepped. That was the whole point of this exercise, wasn't it? she assured herself. She willed herself not to flinch too savagely as he cupped her elbow, the power and strength and sheer male warmth of his hand making her flesh cringe, burn, as he suggested in that cool, polite, easy tone of his, 'The kitchen, I think. I find it by far the nicest room in the house. Do you mind?'

She didn't bother to answer that. What did it matter? She numbly followed where he led. And she didn't blame him for preferring the kitchen. These days, she and her father practically lived in the room, the big Aga stove keeping it warm on even the chilliest nights. She had purloined furniture from the rest of the house, expending time and energy to make at least this room clean and comfortable and bright in a house which had been gradually denuded of anything really saleable.

He was casually dressed now, the faded denims and sleeveless white cotton shirt not detracting a fraction from the lithe power of that perfectly proportioned, very definitely male body of his. In fact, they enhanced it, drawing Christa's unwilling attention to his emphatic masculine beauty.

Beauty? She had never applied that word to any man before and she was appalled by herself. She flicked her eyes away, embarrassed because he must have seen the way she'd been staring at him.

Dragging a chair from under the large scrubbed pine table, she wished, with some sharply honed feminine instinct, that she had had the foresight to scrape her riotous curls back into the pony-tail she sometimes wore around the house and which, according to her father, made her look around twelve years old. But it was too late to do anything about it now, so she fastened her eyes on the bowl of honeysuckle she'd placed on the dresser yesterday.

Donahue said, 'Wine, Christa?' his voice a low throaty purr, smooth as cream.

Compulsively, she lifted her head, meeting his eyes, and that was a mistake. They were strange eyes, magnetic, disturbing...

'With your father's compliments.' He was smiling, a small, very self-possessed smile, as if he knew she found him sexually attractive.

Did she? She had to get a grip on herself. She said, 'Thank you,' very cool, quite impersonal, and was pleased with herself. So what if she found him physically attractive? So nothing. Any woman with eyes would have to admit that much. To deny it would be like trying to say that the Mona Lisa had been badly painted! But that didn't mean to say she found him attractive as a human being. Far from it.

He poured the wine, leaving the glasses in front of her, and perched on the table—close, much too close, one long lithely muscled leg drawn over the other, ankle casually resting against knee.

'I like the way you've decorated this room,' he told her warmly, his eyes touching the pretty floral curtains, the comfortable armchairs covered in the same fabric, the stripped pine cupboards and side tables—inexpensive things, chosen for a homely effect, an oasis in a house that was now little more than a shell.

'Shall we get to the point?' She ignored his attempted pleasantry. 'You wanted to tell me of some so-called business deal you've cooked up with my father.'

She didn't look at him as she spoke, and her words were just as sharply dismissive as she'd intended them to be, a touch of sarcasm giving them bite. She had to keep the upper hand. Had to. She was edgy. She hoped that much didn't show, hoped that her attitude might impress on him the fact that he was dealing with a woman of cool reserve, of common sense, not with someone of her father's gullibility, who would fall over backwards to take up any scheme—no matter how nefarious—to restore his beloved home.

'So that's the way he described it.' Donahue seemed lightly amused, as if he would not have chosen those particular words himself but was willing to give them credence. 'It is one angle, I suppose.'

'I would like you to get to the point,' she repeated tartly, her fingers drumming on the top of the table. 'I don't have time to waste on——'

'Dirty opportunists?' he cut in smoothly, the slithers of ice in the cream giving warning of battle.

'If you like to put it that way—yes.' He had given her no reason to change her original opinion of him. He was up to no good. She met his silver eyes challengingly, encountered a coldness she hadn't met before, and looked away, strangely confused, picking up her glass of wine.

'It was you who chose to put it that way, not I,' he reminded her. 'And while I can understand that you should have felt dubious at six this morning you surely must agree, now, that I was invited here, and for a specific purpose. So, very well, to business.' He used the word as if he suddenly found it distasteful, and levered himself to a standing position, so that he towered over her.

More than ever, she felt threatened. Perhaps he was right, maybe she should give him the benefit of the doubt, hear what he had to say before she judged him. But, despite her intrinsic common sense, in this instance she found she couldn't do any such thing. The very vibes he gave off affected her adversely—an interaction of incompatible chemicals, she supposed, wishing he'd move away.

He did, and she began to breathe more easily again as he stationed himself to stare from one window, the rigidity of back and neck muscles telling of great inner control. But the easiness didn't last for long, just as she had really known it wouldn't, because the breath was knocked out of her lungs when he drawled, 'Ambrose lost a great deal of money last night.'

So she had been right all along. The 'business deal' had to do with a gambling debt. But that didn't lessen the shock. She felt sick. But he wasn't going to know that. She asked tightly, 'How much does he owe you?'

He turned slowly, leaning back against the windowsill, his face in shadow, unreadable. But his eyes were on her, their expression hidden from her, but holding her. He took a long appreciative swallow of wine, still pinning her down with his eyes, then said slowly, distinctly, 'He owes me nothing. He owes a very great deal to Lassiter, the owner of the particular club he was playing at last night. I am in the position to help him, to pay his debts in full—on certain conditions.'

She felt her mouth contract until her lips formed a thin line, pressing against her teeth, as her mental processes rejected his offer out of hand. She knew instinctively that being beholden to this man would be like committing a form of certain suicide.

Positive thinking was what was required now, nothing else. And the whole mess could be a kind of blessing in disguise. For a long time now she had pleaded with her father to sell the Hall, to face the unpalatable fact that there was no way they'd ever be able to afford the upkeep, the necessary structural repairs.

So they could still sell the place, settle the debt, and hopefully there would be enough left over to buy a small house or apartment they could share. And if there wasn't, she would be earning enough to keep them both when her promotion came through—she would be only too delighted to take up her interrupted career.

'I can understand your shock, but wouldn't you like to hear my conditions?'

The oddly gentle voice didn't really impinge on her consciousness; she was simply aware that he had spoken and she raised blank eyes to his, her mind still planning ahead.

He didn't move and his eyes were watchful, very alert, as he told her softly, 'In exchange for discharging your father's debt I would take this house, and in return I would guarantee to restore it, to allow him to live here for his lifetime if he wished to do so, to provide him with an occupation compatible with his standing. Am I making myself clear, Christa?'

She blinked, dragging her unseeing gaze away from her barely touched wine, meeting his unfathomable eyes.

Making himself clear? She supposed he was. And, on the face of it, it sounded generous. To live in the home of his ancestors—as it had been in the days of his youth—had long been her father's unrealistic dream. But she didn't trust Donahue and it was written plainly on her features as she drawled disdainfully, 'You still haven't told me how much Father owes.' For all she knew, it might be merely a fraction of what the house would fetch on the open market. And her father might have jumped at the opportunity of signing the property over so long as he could go on living here as he had done in the old days.

Well, the old days didn't mean much to Christa. The bulk of the estate had already been sold off by the time she was born, the house itself already showing signs of decay at the time of her mother's death. No, Christa was firmly a woman of today, and the future counted more than the past. No way—even if she'd been vaguely tempted by Donahue's strange offer—would she stand by and watch her father sign everything away on a mere sentimental whim.

'I believe that's for him to tell you, not me,' he replied to her question, moving closer, still watching her, poker-faced. 'But I do have one more condition to make.'

'Fire away.' She said it knowing it wouldn't affect the outcome of her decision, and she said it gaily, with a touch of bravado, because, unaccountably, she was feeling nervous again. Not exactly afraid of him, because he couldn't force her and Ambrose to accept a deal that would enable him to gain a mini-mansion, albeit decrepit, plus two acres of prime Hertfordshire land for what would probably amount to a fraction of its true value. No, not exactly afraid, but nearly so; nothing else could explain the panic her body went into whenever he came too close.

'As I'm sure you're intelligent enough to know, the deal I've outlined doesn't need your approval. The property isn't entailed—that was broken back in your grandfather's time—so everything could be settled between Ambrose and myself. However——' He paused, as if looking for words which evaded his hitherto easy command, and Christa mentally conceded that he did have a point there, but only a minor one. She knew her father would listen to what she had to say, not only because they had always been close, but because he was a dyed-in-the-wool traditionalist and, without question, he would see Liddiat Hall as her birthright, allowing her some say in the matter.

So Donahue's statement of fact hadn't given her much to worry about, but what he said next made her feel ill.

'The other contingent condition is that you agree to become my wife.'

Feeling ill didn't last long—the violent lurching in the pit of her stomach quickly gave way to a heady lightness, a feeling of almost hysterical relief.

The man was quite obviously insane! She might have had to argue long and hard to prevent her father from taking up the initial part of the offer, but *this*! This was way over the top and there was no way Ambrose would go along with *that* stipulation!

She began to laugh, softly at first, then almost painfully. Donahue reached out and gripped her arms, dragging her to her feet, and he didn't need to slap her to break the hysteria—all he had to do was touch her to make her completely sober again, horribly aware of the tingling sensation of mind-sharpening tension that contact with him provoked.

'Get lost!' she snapped, her movements deliberately insulting as she hauled herself from his grasp, brushing her arms with her hands as if his touch had defiled her. And when she looked at him his head was high, his cold eyes glittering.

'Don't think that's your last word on the subject, Christa, because, believe me, it isn't.' His breathing was harsh, but controlled, and he turned on his heels and walked out of the room, leaving her feeling as if she had just lived through a nightmare.

CHAPTER THREE

CHRISTA stared at the closed door for long minutes, trying to clear her head of Donahue and his insane offer. Before, she had almost felt a grudging respect for the way his devious mind was working. If he had succeeded in getting Liddiat Hall for a knock-down price he would have seen the renovations as nothing less than a sound investment. That her father would still be living on the premises he would have seen as a necessary evil, an inducement to get the bargain he had seen within his grasp.

But by adding the other stipulation he had shown himself to be bordering on the crazy. What sane man would want to marry a woman he'd never set eyes on before this morning, a woman, moreover, who'd clearly shown him she didn't trust him an inch? And what sane man would expect any woman to agree to such a preposterous idea?

Struggling to dismiss him from her mind, she tried to focus on what she had to say to her father. The Donahue joke apart—and that was the only way she could regard it—the house had to be sold, the debt discharged and more sensible living arrangements made. And hopefully the inevitable loss of the family home would put her father off gambling for life, bring him at last to his senses.

She ran him to earth in the deserted stable block. She had guessed he would be here. He had haunted the place for weeks after her mother's death, she remembered, drawing what comfort he could from his work with the hunters he bred and trained.

But the horses had all long since been sold, following one or two disastrous business misjudgements, and the work which had taken up so much of his life had left a space behind which, Christa recognised with hindsight, he had attempted to fill by gambling—especially after she had left to make her home in London, finding work opportunities there that this area could not match.

He looked up as he heard her approach, his smile wary.

'I take it you've had a word with Ross? He's gone, by the way. Asked me to tell you he'd be in touch.'

She was glad he had gone, far more than glad. And if he tried to get in touch she'd make damn sure she wasn't available!

Taking the gentle line, she tucked her arm through her father's.

'Let's talk.'

'Yes, of course.' He was anxious to comply, walking with her to the old stone mounting block. Too anxious perhaps, for he sat when she sat, the evening sun highlighting the pleading look in his eyes.

'About that debt——' She held up a hand to stem whatever it was he had been about to say. Now wasn't the time for garbled explanations, hasty reassurances— she'd heard too many of those in the past. Nor was it the time for recriminations. What was done couldn't be undone. The future was the only thing that counted.

'We'll pay it,' she began levelly. 'The house will have to go, of course. I'm sorry.' She reached for his hand, smiling into his troubled face. She felt a pang of compassion—she couldn't help herself. She knew how much his family home meant to him.

As a very small child he had taught her all she knew about her Liddiat ancestors, weaving stories around each and every one of the family portraits, around the collection of campaign medals won by Liddiat men in battles as long ago as Waterloo, thrilling her with tales of high adventure attached to souvenirs from places as distant as China, the Sudan, the Russia of the Tsars, teaching her the history of the Liddiats whose carved effigies now slept in peace in the ancient estate church.

Now the portraits were sold, along with the collections, and the church was never used, its single silvery-toned bell silenced forever.

And she knew how he must feel—that the sale of the house itself, and the neglected gardens which were all that was left of an estate that had once covered a thousand acres, would be an admission of his failed stewardship.

His upbringing had not equipped him to deal with late-twentieth-century life. For centuries Liddiat males had run the prosperous estate, money no object and labour cheap and plentiful. But the feudal hierarchy had finally and irretrievably broken down with the advent of the Second World War and Ambrose had no head for business, was a throwback, unable to cope in the harsher climate that had swept over the old landed families of Europe.

And, in his own way, he had tried to stem the effects of rising costs and diminishing returns by gambling. But they had to look to the future now, no point in looking over their shoulders into the past. She had to make him see that. She repeated softly, 'This house must be sold, you have to see that.'

'The house isn't mine to sell.'

His words came as a vicious bombshell, wrecking her pattern of thought, causing chaos.

'Why not?' Her lips formed the words stiffly, automatically, which was stupid because she thought she already knew the answer.

'I owed a hell of a lot to Lassiter.' He looked at her painfully, and then quickly away again, 'Then I hit that lucky streak I've been waiting for for months, won back all I owed. Went on, using Liddiat Hall as a stake——'

'Why?' The single word was a howled plea for sanity. Christa pushed her hands through the silvery strands of her hair. 'Why go on if you'd covered your debts?'

'Because I was on a winning streak.' He looked at her with bleak eyes.

'And then you lost,' Christa guessed acidly, at the end of her patience.

He admitted, 'And went on losing.' He passed a shaky hand over his forehead, the perspiration there having nothing to do with the waning power of the sun. 'Donahue had arrived by then—he—well, he could see I'd got out of my depth. He offered to bail me out on certain conditions.'

So that was how it had come about. Christa heaved a shaky sigh. She wanted to pack her bags and walk out, but knew she couldn't do it.

'I've heard the conditions,' she said bitterly, demanding, 'Did he bother to tell you that I was to be part of the package? That before he agrees to pay your debts I have to agree to marry him!' She was doing her best to keep hysteria out of her voice, to stay calm, and she fully expected the man beside her to deny all knowledge of such a monstrous suggestion.

But he said in a low voice, 'Yes, I know.'

'And you would have gone along with that?' She could hardly believe she wasn't living through a nightmare. 'So you get to keep the house for your lifetime, live here without a worry in the world—if the roof leaks, never mind, Donahue will get it fixed! And I get to marry that...' Words failed her. She turned furious eyes on him. 'I'm the dispensable asset around here—the little matter of marrying me off to some freak doesn't come into it!'

'Christa! It's not like that!' He made to rise then sagged back on to the stone again. 'I didn't want it this way.'

'Then you should stay home at night,' she told him coldly. 'Not gamble away money you haven't got with con-men and criminals! Or if you can't kick the damned habit, go somewhere where the players are at least gentlemen!'

'Donahue's not——'

'Not a gentleman,' Christa put in sharply. 'Do you think I don't know that. I have met him!' she reminded him with bitter sarcasm, recalling too vividly those mocking silver eyes, that oh so casual air of arrogance— all the more potent for not being strutted. 'And what does he want with me?' she demanded waspishly. 'If I was ever fool enough to agree to marry him, he'd soon wake up to the fact that he hadn't got himself a bargain!'

'If you married him, Christa, you'd be safe for the rest of your life, you'd have everything you'd ever wanted.'

'And what about love, respect?' she flared. 'Or don't those things matter any more?'

'Love grows,' he told her wearily. 'And as for respect, well, Ross is already highly respected, besides being extremely wealthy. For a start, he owns a string of high-class restaurants——'

'Is that supposed to impress me?' she grated. 'Well, I can tell you one thing—I won't marry him, not even to save this place for you. Listen——' she was standing now, her hands placed firmly on her slender hips '—give him this place. Walk away from it. With me.' Unconsciously, her voice softened. 'I can earn enough to support both of us. We could find a flat to rent and my old job's waiting for me—and I'm fairly certain I'll be offered promotion in the near future.'

Whatever her father's failings, she did love him. Though at the moment she couldn't think why! And they could make a good life together, he might even be able to find a part-time job to help fill his time. In any case, they were in this mess together and they'd get out of it together. Rise above it.

She thought she had won him over to her way of thinking, but that was only during those few meagre seconds before she saw him stiffen, saw him push himself to his feet, heard him say rawly, 'It's a nice idea, but it won't work. What I owe can in no way be covered by the value of this place, and I don't even legally own it now, remember? If I handed it over to Donahue, as it stands, and he paid my debts, he'd lose hand over fist. There would be more money outstanding than either of us could ever hope to repay. And it would probably mean prison for me. But if you can't accommodate him, Christa, I'll understand.'

She watched him stumble from the stableyard, her eyes wild. She simply could not bring herself to think of the deep implication of what he had said—but she had to force herself to face it . . .

'Father!' She caught up with him as he was entering the house. 'Wait!' The raw urgency in her voice stopped him in his tracks, his shoulders bowed. 'What did you mean about prison?'

And he turned slowly, facing her but not looking at her, and she asked huskily, 'Tell me exactly what would happen if I refused to marry Donahue.' The house didn't matter, not now, he could take it and burn it for all she cared. Nothing mattered but that last deadly stipulation. The very thought of being married against her will made her feel nauseous.

'He would not pay the debt, it's as simple as that.'

'And then?' she persisted, her face pale.

'And then I would lose this house, everything. And I would almost certainly face a prison sentence.'

'Why prison?' She felt as if her legs were about to give way under her, but she had to be strong—she had to know the full facts, and then do something about them.

He began to move away towards the stairs, very slowly, like a man in a trance, and his voice was thick as he told her, 'When I knew I'd lost the Hall I had to try to get it back—win it back. I used the Home Farm as a further stake.'

'You did what?' She followed him, taking his arm roughly. 'Have you gone mad! Home Farm was sold back in the Sixties, to pay death duties when Grandfather died!'

'I know it, you know it. Lassiter didn't. I lost a property that wasn't mine to lose and that's why I'll go behind bars if Donahue doesn't pay that debt.'

And then, in the aching silence, she heard the phone ring. Slowly, dazedly, she walked to the kitchen. The instrument was on the wall, tucked in beside the dresser, and she knew, even before she lifted the receiver, who would be on the other end.

'Donahue.' The voice was crisp, no undertones, purely businesslike. 'I'll give you dinner tomorrow night. I'll pick you up at eight. I'm sure, by now, that you'll agree we have certain matters to discuss.'

The line went dead. Christa stared at the gently buzzing instrument for long paralysed moments before setting it back in place.

Then she started to shake all over. The nightmare had switched into second gear.

CHAPTER FOUR

CHRISTA sat in ungiving silence in the sleek black Lotus Elan. Ross Donahue wasn't saying anything either, his eyes fixed unwaveringly on the road. And that was just as well, she simmered. Just as well. One smart-aleck remark out of him would have her blowing a fuse. It was all she could do to hang on to her self-control as it was.

At last he drew the car to a halt in a quiet street in Mayfair, and turned to her. Silver eyes looked black as night in the muddled light from street lamps and passing traffic.

'Hungry?' he asked quietly, sliding round in his seat, half facing her now.

'No.' She turned her head, staring stonily out of the window. She didn't want to look at him, to eat with him, to have anything to do with him. But she knew they had to thrash this thing out. She had to talk to him, try to make him see sense. It was the only reason she'd been ready and waiting when he'd picked her up at eight.

'Pity.' There was a dryness in his voice. 'They're expecting us.'

'Who?' Unable to resist the temptation, she swung around, peering over her shoulder to the elegant façade of the building they were parked in front of. A small discreetly lit sign read 'Tinkers' in gilded Italian script. She supposed it to be an expensive eating house—one of his, even—and the slight shrug of her shoulders announced as clearly as any words that she wasn't impressed. Wouldn't be impressed by anything about him.

She wasn't hungry. All she wanted to do was to try to persuade this man to her point of view. Where it was done was a matter of supreme indifference to her.

A smooth, intensely controlled movement had him out of the car, clipping sardonically, 'Great!' and as he walked around to her side of the classy vehicle she could see by the set of his wide dinner-suited shoulders, the severe cast of the sculpted features, that he was far from pleased.

Well, the sooner he realised that she didn't exist to please him, now or ever, the better for all concerned, she thought rebelliously as he opened the door, inviting her to exit. And she'd be damned if she allowed him to gain the upper hand in this or any other situation.

Her head held haughtily high, she stood aside as Ross was greeted by a uniformed doorman.

'Park the car would you, Edgeley, please?' He tossed the doorman a bunch of keys then his hand was on her elbow, urging her forward, and it was all Christa could do to contain herself. She didn't want him near her, never mind touching her, and the only way to stop herself from spitting and clawing like a wild cat was to cling tightly on to her dignity. To get through this evening at all she had to have something to cling to, and her pride and her dignity seemed to be the only things she had left in this nightmare.

'Good evening, Mr Donahue, Miss Liddiat.' The dark-suited, middle-aged man's smile was reverential, his gleaming shoes clicking on the deep red floor tiles as he moved to greet them. Beyond his shoulder Christa could see into the restaurant itself. The same deep red colour predominated, lightened by the overhead glitter of crystal chandeliers, by gleaming silverware and sparkling glass.

A cocooning womb of luxury, she thought edgily, patronised by the very sophisticated, those discerning enough and wealthy enough to afford the very best in food and wine and service.

'Christa, meet Alec Canfield,' Ross said and she dipped her head slightly, acknowledging Canfield's smile, his openly curious eyes, feeling too uptight to manage much of a smile herself. 'Alec manages my London restaurant,' Ross went on to explain in a softly drawling voice that sent shivers skittering up and down Christa's spine. 'Though we'll be losing him shortly. He'll be going Stateside to manage Tinkers New York when it opens.'

Christa forced another pallid smile, trying to look interested for Alec Canfield's sake. It wasn't his fault that his boss was a devious monster.

'Sorry to have dragged you back,' Alec Canfield murmured, but Ross cut through his apology with a downward chop of one strong yet elegantly made hand.

'You did the right thing. I take it Pierre is here?'

'Very much so. Thursday night's little misunderstanding left him in no doubt that you meant what you said. He knows he'll never work as a top chef anywhere in the world if he strays again.'

If this little interchange was meant to impress then Christa wasn't interested. She already knew that Ross Donahue had a ruthless streak ten miles wide and she felt sorry for Pierre, no matter what he'd done to earn his boss's displeasure.

Pinning a rigidly bored expression on her face, she walked woodenly towards the restaurant, but a hand on her arm halted her, making her grind her teeth.

'This way,' Ross told her, then, to Canfield, 'We'll eat in half an hour.'

Bemused violet eyes took in the platinum-sheened lift on the far side of the elegant, hushed foyer and she stiffened as Ross guided her into it. But she forced herself to try to relax as the doors of the silvery metal box closed them in.

He told her, 'We'll have dinner in my apartment. When I'm in London I live above the shop, as it were—it's convenient. And we'll be more private.'

A good idea on the whole, she reassured herself staunchly. She didn't want what she had to say to him to be overheard by others.

'I can spare you one hour, Mr Donahue. It should give us enough time to get this mess sorted out.'

'As far as I'm concerned, it already is. Nothing could be more straightforward,' he commented with aggravating smoothness as the lift doors opened on a muted hiss. She tried to judge his mood and gave up the attempt. His face was deadpan.

He ushered her through a door on the opposite side of the vestibule and took her coat, and Christa was glad she'd gone to so much trouble over her appearance. She knew she'd achieved the effect she'd aimed for.

Richly sleek black satin sheathed her slender body from neck to ankle, the severity of the style lightened only by the single strand of pearls that gleamed softly on the pale skin at the base of her throat. Silver-gilt curls were tamed tonight, coiled heavily on the top of her head, her only concession to make-up a shimmer of coral on her lips, the merest touch of deep grey eye-shadow.

She had wanted to present a controlled, poised exterior to counteract the panicky feeling inside, and that, she noted with an inner flicker of satisfaction, was exactly what she had done. His silver eyes, as they had travelled her greyhound lines, had been quite emotionless, almost uninterested, quite without that terrifying glint of sexual interest she had noted on previous occasions. And that was the way she wanted it. With any luck he would already be regretting the infamous deal he had set up with her father.

'Can I give you a drink?' A small crooked smile rendered his question just about civil and she shook her head, sitting in a soft grey leather armchair, her eyes wandering the room as he poured for himself.

It was expensively, tastefully furnished but it said nothing of the man himself. It could have been part of a suite in an exorbitantly priced hotel. But she didn't need personal trappings to help her read his personality, she decided. She already had enough to go on.

Christa firmly believed that the best form of defence was attack and tonight she wasn't going to pull her punches. So when he turned and she saw the abstemious amount of sherry he had given himself, she raised one fly-away eyebrow and remarked in the most condescending tone she could manage, 'And I thought all gamblers were hard-drinking men!'

He was very still for a moment and then some nameless emotion made his eyes opaque as he countered, 'My God—you need taking down a peg or two!' And, just for a moment of time, fury stared out of his eyes but Christa met the deadly gaze head on, her chin lifting.

And then all expression left his face—it was like watching a slate being wiped clean as, indolently, he let himself down into the chair which was a twin to the one she was using, one leanly elegant leg crossed over the other.

'To set the record straight, I don't drink when I'm driving and I'll be taking you back later tonight. And I never gamble, it's a mug's game.'

That had to be the most blatant lie Christa had ever heard! The rosebud mouth primmed as she controlled her temper and clipped out icily, 'Then how did you come to be at Lassiter's that night? Don't tell me—let me guess. You'd simply wandered in off the street under the impression it was a temperance hall.' She sucked in her breath, sickened by him and what he represented. 'And my father just happened to be there, and you watched him get himself in deep trouble, and you took over, cooking up this twisted deal of yours. It wouldn't surprise me in the least if you and Lassiter——' she spat the word out delicately, for the very sound of it on her lips was distasteful to her '—hadn't rigged the whole thing.'

She fully expected his anger at that taunt—was ready for it. His laughter threw her. Instinctively, her hand flew to her throat, her fingers touching the milky coolness of the pearls she wore.

His eyes narrowed, following her gesture.

'Your home is falling apart around your ears.' There was no trace of laughter now, only of distaste in the way his mouth twisted downwards. 'The creditors are hammering on the door, yet you deck yourself in pearls and designer gowns. I wonder why?' He folded his arms across his chest, his eyes watching her with glimmering intensity. 'Too selfish to give up the trappings of society? Or would it be beneath the dignity of a Liddiat of Liddiat Hall to appear in public in chain-store clothes and fake jewellery?'

She would have given anything to be able to sweep out of the room, to hit him for his patronising tone, but there were things to be discussed and the arrival of a white-coated waiter had her pinned in her chair, fuming.

The pearls had been her mother's, given to her on her wedding day by *her* mother. The necklace was the only piece of her mother's scant collection of jewellery left and under no circumstances would Christa allow it to be sold. It was all she had left of her mother and she had worn it tonight because she had superstitiously felt they might bring her closer, make her feel she wasn't so alone—that somehow the gentle, beautiful person who had died ten years ago would be watching over her with that same generous unpossessive love.

And the dress was one of Tania's designs, part of the small but exclusive evening hire range. And when Christa had gone to the boutique this morning, explaining what she wanted, Tania had refused to take the fee, insisting that the hire of an evening gown for just one night must be regarded as a legitimate perk. But when Christa had tried it on the other girl had tilted her auburn head consideringly, 'You look beautiful but remote. A touch frigid, darling. It would take a brave man to approach you while you're wearing that. Sure you wouldn't prefer to take the flame chiffon?'

But cool and remote had been the effect she'd wanted, so she'd stuck with the black and had no regrets at all. And if he chose to believe she'd paid the earth for it, then that was fine by her. And her eyes were very slightly, coolly amused as he stood up, motioning her to the table at the other end of the room.

'I'm not hungry,' she stated coldly, playing the part she had assigned herself.

'Christa.' He sounded almost weary. 'We need to talk and we need to eat. Why not try to be civilised about it?'

She lifted one slender shoulder in a couldn't-care-less shrug and paced with unwilling slowness to the table near the window, watching with eyes that glittered with sudden unstoppable panic as the waiter discreetly withdrew.

Seated opposite Ross, Christa felt perspiration dew her short curling upper lip, gather in the centre of her palms. It was a warm June night, but not that warm! She was letting him make her nervous. He was getting to her, and she had more backbone than to let him do that to her, surely?

Swallowing down the panicky butterflies in her stomach which seemed set to rise to her throat, choking her, she found her most chilling tone and used it. 'Father and I will hand Liddiat Hall over to you, unconditionally, if and when you pay his debt.' She began spreading rich venison pâté over a slice of hot crisp toast with what she hoped would appear as cool indifference, unprepared for his cutting response.

'The Hall isn't your father's to give. He used it as a stake, lost it to Lassiter—and a great deal more, which he has no hope of covering.'

She knew that, of course, but he wanted the Hall, didn't he? Acquiring it had been the least objectionable of his conditions. It looked as though he was intent on throwing her offer back in her face. But she had to try again, try to make him see reason.

'You were prepared to restore the house, to allow my father to live there for as long as he wished—also to guarantee that he never again had a moment's financial worry. Now that, as I see it, would be costly, also most inconvenient should he happen to live to a very great age! What we're doing is simply offering you the Hall, with no strings attached. I'm quite capable of giving

Father an adequate home, and, as you want the Hall——'

'No, Christa.' The disclaimer fell curtly. 'As I've already tried to explain, the house, the land, and a great deal more, was lost to Lassiter. To the club, if you like, which Lassiter owns. When I arrived your father was in a blue funk. I merely took over.' Even white teeth bit into a slice of pâté-spread toast with every sign of enjoyment. 'I suggested a way out of his—predicament?' One brow arched mockingly as if his choice of word had been a sop to her sensibilities, and she felt colour crawl over her skin.

'You don't need to patronise me,' she snapped, knowing she was losing control of the situation.

'Nor protect you, I suppose. Very well.' He reached for another slice of toast. 'As I said, Ambrose was frightened; he didn't know where he was at.' He forked up a little of the crisp shredded salad, apparently unaware of the disgusted glitter in Christa's eyes. 'So I promised to pay what he owed, provided a private deal could be struck. I am not particularly interested in owning Liddiat Hall, but I am interested in owning you—as my wife.'

'But why? For God's sake why!' Her strangled question was a cross between a gulp and a groan. Ross ignored it.

He took away her barely touched starter and lifted the silver cover from a dish the waiter had left on the heated trolley. He brought the poached salmon to the table, his voice totally devoid of expression as he told her, 'Let's just concern ourselves with the facts. That Ambrose owes far more than he could ever hope to repay, that he faces a probable prison sentence. That I have agreed to pay his debt in full, to restore the Hall and allow him to remain there—also to look after him financially. All this, provided a certain condition is met.'

'You disgust me!' she grated, all pretence at cool reserve deserting her now. Her father might be weak, a fool when the gambling bug bit—but this creature was something else! A worm, a low, disgusting worm! He didn't know the meaning of honour and he wouldn't recognise a scruple if it bit him on the nose!

'I think I can live with that.'

The mockery behind that remark brought her head up high, and she repeated *'Why?'* more firmly this time. But he chose to misunderstand her.

'Because I don't like the type of men who run such clubs. They get sleek and fat on the weakness of others. Besides,' he handed her a laden plate, 'I know your father, in a manner of speaking. We have met on various occasions. I like him—I wanted to help him out of a tight spot.'

'I meant,' Christa snapped through clenched teeth, 'why bring me into it? Why the hell should you want to own me, as you so charmingly put it? What possible use could I be to you?'

'The greatest possible use.' His features quite impassive, Ross leaned back in his chair, not a flicker to betray any interest as she pushed the food away, grimacing at the succulent fish, the tiny new potatoes and spring vegetables as if he had given her a plate of compost to eat. Her eyes sought his, tried to read what went on inside that well-shaped skull, but he returned her gaze with a blandness that made her grind her teeth with frustration.

His home had told her nothing about him, and neither did his face. Apart from the occasional brief flash of anger, a glint of that devilish mockery, his features were expressionless, telling her nothing. It was as if the real Ross Donahue had hidden himself behind this suave façade a long time ago. Christa found that the most frightening thing about him.

'Well?' she goaded acidly. 'What use?'

Smiling slightly, like a cat who had discovered the Christmas turkey left unattended, he forked up a morsel of fish. 'As my wife you would be a very definite social asset. We would live at Liddiat Hall—an excellent address, I believe—provided your father didn't object, of course,' he added drily. 'And you would give me entrée into that closed shop—upper-middle-class society. The Liddiats are an old and respected county family and as your husband I would be accepted.' He laid down his fork, silver eyes glinting with something unfathomable as they held hers.

'In my experience, achievement, wealth, business acumen, are not enough. A threadbare Liddiat would be welcomed in certain circles where a silk-suited Donahue would be very politely ignored, shown the door.'

So as well as being an unscrupulous worm, he was a whingeing social climber! She didn't think any such creatures were left in existence. She snarled, 'I wouldn't marry you if you held a gun to my head!'

'Too plebeian for you?' he enquired softly, dangerously.

She sniped back, 'Too right!'

'You can't forget your background, your class, can you? The last Liddiat of Liddiat Hall!' A touch of frost in the tone now, a twitch of a muscle at the side of his mouth. So she was getting to him, was she? The idea of that made her feel on a high, strangely exultant, as if she was at last getting to grips with the man behind the mask. Though why she should want to was something she didn't stop to think about. She said cuttingly, 'Got it in one. And why should I, in any case?' She was at last almost enjoying herself. He had frightened, worried and appalled her; it was time she got a little of her own back, got under his thick hide for a change.

If he thought she was refusing his outrageous proposal—if what he had said to her could be dignified by such a word—because she was a snob of the first water, then that was fine by her! He obviously had a chip on his shoulder a foot thick, and if she could add to its weight then she damned well would, just for the heck of it!

Adrenalin flowing well now, she told him, 'I won't marry you. I couldn't touch scum like you with a ten-foot pole!' She saw his face harden, his eyes change colour until they were black, so that she almost regretted her taunts.

She wasn't a snob, far from it. True, the Liddiats had a documented history that went back hundreds of years and the stories of her ancestors had always fascinated her. But that was as far as it went. She had little time for the so-called county set herself and happened to believe that each individual stood or fell on his or her own merits, regardless of background. The more recent Liddiat history was nothing to be proud of, anyway, and she had been happiest when living away from home, making a worthwhile career for herself.

From the look in his eyes she had undoubtedly drawn blood, but he answered levelly enough, 'If you mean what you say, the debt is firmly back in your father's corner. But if that is what you want...'

His voice tailed off deliberately and Christa felt physically ill as he went on coldly, 'Even the sale of the house and everything left in it——' his eyes fell appraisingly on the pearls around her throat and her skin crawled with sensation, as if he had touched her '—wouldn't save your father from gaol. Do you think he could stand the shock, the humiliation? I don't.'

He didn't need to spell it out. She knew her father would never survive the shame, the public scandal.

A trial, a term behind bars, might not actually kill him—but would spending the remainder of his life feeling disgraced and ashamed be much better than death?

The breath seemed to solidify in her lungs, and her heart was pattering crazily beneath her ribs. And whether it was because she was affected by the thought of her father in prison, or by the thought of this predator as her husband, she couldn't have said to save her life.

'I must have time to think it over,' she muttered stonily.

'No,' he answered patiently, gently, as if to a child. 'Ambrose can't have told you, but unless Lassiter receives my cheque by nine o'clock on Monday morning he will initiate proceedings against your father. Do you really intend to stand by and see that happen? If his public disgrace doesn't mean anything to you, then yours might. Some of it is bound to brush off. So you see, Christa, if your answer's no, then that is precisely what will happen. If it's yes——' he steepled his fingers, silver eyes hooded, enigmatic '—then my cheque will be delivered to Lassiter at exactly nine on Monday morning. As for the rest—for your keeping your side of the bargain—I shall have to trust to Liddiat honour, won't I?' His upper lip curled derisively and Christa shuddered.

'I'd make you a rotten wife.' And he could take that as a threat if he liked, a declaration of intent, but she was giving him fair warning and still trying to wriggle out of the horrific mess she was in.

He replied, aggravating her still further, 'Even the worst of wives can be tamed. One way or another. Try again.'

Tears of frustrated rage spiked her dark lashes. There was no moving this man. He didn't know the meaning of common sense, of decency.

She got stiffly to her feet, her head high, her dignity the only thing she had left.

'I would like to go now. Tell me, Mr Donahue, would you really throw Father to the wolves?'

She knew what his answer would be, but it was worth a try. Her heart pounded uncomfortably as she waited for his reply, but he had no way of knowing that. Her Liddiat genes held her head high, her spine erect, her eyes cool.

He got to his feet, his face a polite mask.

'Yes. Without a second thought.'

'I see.' She reached for her slim black suede bag. 'Then in that case, I have no option but to accept your proposal.'

She made herself turn and walk slowly to the door, every pore of her skin aware of how close he was as he followed her.

If he touched her she would scream the place down. Stinging sensations already ran over her skin, along every vein, as if his hands were claiming her body in fact, and not only in her own fevered imagination.

CHAPTER FIVE

AMBROSE had been keeping out of Christa's way. He was thoroughly and deservedly ashamed of himself but that knowledge did nothing to help her to come to terms with what lay ahead of her, with what she was going to have to pay for her father's comfort and freedom. She ought to have let him stew, let him pay for his own stupidity, but, even in her greatest moments of doubt, she knew she could never have done that.

She loved her father too much to refuse to help him. Besides, she tried to console herself, there was always divorce. She would make Donahue such a poisonous wife that he would be only too happy to be rid of her. That this attitude wasn't exactly ethical was something she wasn't prepared to consider.

Christa, crossing the shabby hall, her arms piled with dusters and polish tins, heard the telephone ring in the kitchen and stopped in her tracks.

A scowl darkened her small face. It would be Donahue, damn him, confirming the plans for this evening. So she didn't hurry to answer it and when she plucked the shrilling instrument from the wall her voice, as she intoned, 'Liddiat Hall. May I help you?' was undiluted acid.

'Chris? You entertaining royalty to lunch, or something?' a lightly amused baritone enquired facetiously and her hands relaxed, so that the knuckles weren't white any more, and she smiled for the first time in days.

'Howard! You caught me at a bad moment.'

54

'Bad mood, don't you mean?'

She grinned. Her bad moods were rare but when they did occur they could be traumatic and Howard had been on the receiving end of one or two, way back in their childhood days. They had known each other forever, had been part of the same set—he was one of the oldest friends she had.

'Will you have dinner with me tonight?' he went on. 'We could go up to town, or try the nosh at the local. It's under new management and I hear the food's good.'

Christa put the dusters she'd been clutching down on the dresser, settling down for a natter, which she hoped would go some way towards taking her mind off her future.

'What's wrong? Has...' She searched her mind for the name of his latest lady. 'Has Magda walked out on you?'

'Helen,' he corrected. 'Magda was months ago. I need a sympathetic shoulder to lean on.'

That figured. Christa smiled into space. Their friendship was such that they automatically flew to each other when their love-lives went wrong. Not that Christa had had many men-friends, and certainly none of them had been serious. In fact, on more than one occasion, she had co-opted Howard to play the part of the heavy boyfriend in order to frighten off a too persistent would-be lover. And that gave her a very good idea...

'Howard,' she crooned, the smile in her voice as thick as cream, 'I can't make tonight, Father's invited some guy for dinner. Do me a favour and give me some moral support? Black tie, seven-thirty for eight?'

'Will do,' Howard agreed, asking, 'Who is this guy? Anyone I know?'

'Shouldn't think so,' Christa dismissed airily. Howard's family had money, old money, oozing out of their pores, and since he had left university Howard had helped run the prosperous family estate. The only people he really knew were the landed gentry—huntin', shootin' and fishin' types—and Ross Donahue wasn't one of them. Although he was itching to ape them! And she wasn't going to tell Howard the truth, not yet, because she didn't even want to think about it.

As she replaced the receiver, her mouth formed a feline smile. Ross would not be pleased to meet Howard tonight when he turned up for the dinner-party he had instigated, making the arrangements with her father and leaving him to break the unwelcome news. It had been arranged, according to her shame-faced parent, for the sole purpose of settling the arrangements for the forthcoming wedding. A subject Christa could only view with dread.

And Ross would be doubly displeased when she, with Howard's connivance or without it, made it plain where her affections lay. It would, she hoped, give him a foretaste of what life would be like married to a woman he'd had to blackmail into accepting him! She also hoped it would give him profound indigestion.

As she dressed for dinner she found herself smiling at her reflected image in the mirror. She almost felt relaxed, a state of mind that had totally eluded her since he had put forward his foul conditions.

She was sensible enough to know that the vaguely euphoric mood wouldn't last. Very soon now the future, which at the moment was simply a dark and ominous threat, would become hateful reality.

But this evening should prove to be a little light relief and go some way to showing Ross that, although he had the upper hand at the moment, he wouldn't have everything his own way during what she devoutly hoped would be their short-lived marriage.

She wasn't going to be led to the altar all wan and martyred—she had a damn sight more backbone than that. She had been backed into a corner but she wasn't going to passively stay there!

When her father had broken the news that Ross had invited himself to dinner tonight her instinct had been to absent herself, leaving them to forage for themselves. But somehow she'd changed her mind, she didn't quite know why, and had elected to throw as grand a dinner-party as she could manage.

'We'd have been more comfortable in the kitchen,' Ambrose remarked as Christa flicked a stray piece of fluff from his ancient dinner-jacket.

Christa ignored that. She couldn't explain why she'd decided to go the whole hog when she didn't know the reason herself.

But the lofty dining-room, when she entered it, her father tagging reluctantly along behind her, gave her some satisfaction.

Thankfully it was Saturday, her day off, so she had been able to spend time cleaning and polishing, dragging a bruised old gate-legged table from the attics, gathering pine cones and splitting logs for the fire which now crackled in the carved stone fireplace.

The judicious use of a variety of patchwork quilts tossed over the two long sofas disguised the fact that they were threadbare, the stuffing poking out in places. And the scuffed table had been covered with one of her grandmother's lace cloths, and she herself was looking every inch the perfect hostess in a floor-length wine-coloured velvet skirt and an oyster-coloured heavy satin sleeveless top which boasted a tantalising deep V neckline.

'Who else are we expecting?' Ambrose frowned at the four covers on the oval table, the ivory-coloured old lace going some way to disguising the fact that the china and glass, though good, didn't match and that the silver wasn't.

'Howard Mortmain,' Christa informed him airily, her ears pricking at the sound of a vehicle spattering the gravel of the drive. 'Maybe that's him now.'

She hoped it wasn't Donahue. She needed a moment to prime Howard on his part for this evening and she flicked her father an uninterested shrug as he grumbled, 'That's not a good idea. Donahue expressly mentioned a private meeting, just the three of us,' and rushed out to open the door.

She didn't much care what her father thought about her plans for the evening. She wasn't in the mood to give him much consideration—it was his fault entirely that she was in this unholy mess.

For once luck was with her and it was Howard. He climbed out of the new Range Rover, hurrying towards the house because the evening had turned grey, spots of rain riding on the back of a chilly wind.

He looked even more handsome than she remembered, his wayward blond hair slicked down for the occasion, sherry-coloured eyes warm and affectionate in a face that was too perfect for its owner's good. His family's wealth and status, allied to his own fantastic looks, were responsible for his troubles with women. They all threw themselves at his feet and he couldn't resist them, but they usually walked out on him when they learned that he had no plans for buying that hoped-for plain gold ring.

'Chris!' Strong arms enfolded her in a bear-like hug. 'How long has it been? Four months? Six?'

'Must be,' Christa concurred, extricating herself with difficulty. It had been five months since she had last seen Howard. It had been January and she had already been back at home for a month, so she had known exactly what difficulties her father was in regarding his finances. Huddled in her old sheepskin, laden down with shopping, she had met Howard on the village street, glad to accept his offer of a lift home. But she hadn't been in the mood to accept his invitation to a dinner-dance the following week. There had been too many financial worries pressing on her mind. She would have been poor company.

Now, aware that her hateful husband-to-be would be arriving at any moment, she tucked her hand through the crook of his arm and began to re-mount the steps.

'Howard, would you do me another favour?' Wide violet eyes, limpid between thick dark lashes, were hard to resist and Howard placed a hand over her tiny one.

'Anything, Chris, you know that.'

Never one to use twenty words when two would do, Christa instructed, 'Pretend you're madly in love with me, just for this one evening.'

'Shouldn't be too taxing.' His warm eyes twinkled. 'Why?'

'I'll tell you some other time,' Christa promised airily, sweeping Howard towards the dining-room.

Her father, his head set at a bellicose angle, grunted, 'Evening, Mortmain. Sherry?' This gruffness was his way of letting Christa know exactly how displeased he was by the addition to the guest list of one.

Tough, thought Christa, nursing the glass her father had handed her without a word, and wriggling closer to Howard as he joined her on the sofa because, suddenly, she felt he was her only ally in a topsy-turvy, antagonistic world.

As the minutes crept by Christa listened in desultory fashion to the conversation between the two men. They had shared interests, the same sort of background, they knew the same people.

Ambrose quickly forgot his annoyance and was picking up on the local news, but she noticed how often his puzzled eyes strayed to her, as if he was asking himself questions and couldn't find any answers.

Howard's arm was draped around her shoulders now. His fingers felt hot and heavy on the cool skin of her naked arm. She tried to ease away, but he pulled her closer, turning to look down into her eyes with a look of devotion which had her marvelling at his acting ability. She ought to have told him to lay off the histrionics until Ross arrived, but she hadn't thought about it.

And it began to seem as if Ross wouldn't come. Her ears were actually hurting from straining to catch the sounds of his arrival. She knew she was getting more uptight with each passing moment and that something remarkably like a lump of disappointment had settled in her stomach.

But she couldn't actually want him to come, could she? She pursed her full lips with an inner denial of any such idiocy and stared blankly at her father who had obviously asked her a question she hadn't heard. And then there was the unmistakable clunk of a closing car door—they all heard it at the same time and Christa's heart lightened, she felt it whoosh upwards, and she started to rise.

But Howard held her back and Ambrose, already halfway across the room, said, 'Stay where you are, I'll let him in,' which was understandable, Christa thought weakly, subsiding back into her seat. A strange mixture of excitement and panic was doing unwelcome things to her insides—due, she knew, to the anticipation of letting Ross know that life with her would not be a bed of roses.

Her father would want to speak to Donahue first, to prime him. He would not want the reasons behind the shot-gun wedding to be bruited around the county, as they would be if Howard got an inkling of what was going on. So thankfully, due to her own quick thinking in inviting Howard here tonight, there would be no nauseous talk of wedding arrangements!

'Relax,' Howard said into her ear. 'You're like a cat on hot bricks.'

And who wouldn't be, in her situation, Christa thought grimly. But she forced a painful smile and Howard said, 'That's better.' He tilted her chin with his index finger and placed his mouth on hers, his lips moving slowly as he asked softly, 'How am I doing?'

'What?' She pulled away from his kiss, resisting the insulting impulse to rub her hand across her mouth. It was like incest. Howard was like the brother she had always wanted and never had; there had never been any-thing remotely romantic between them.

'The loving game,' he murmured huskily. 'I could get used to it.'

'Oh!' Her lips parted, making a rosy circle, her eyes wide and shocked, and he took advantage of the lapse of memory that had caused her to forget she had actually invited him to come on heavy, and kissed her soundly, creating a jumble of sensations that whirled into complete and utter disorder as she heard her father's staged cough, rough with embarrassment.

Her poise completely shattered, she wriggled out of Howard's arms. Ross had to have seen what would have appeared to any onlooker to be a wildly passionate embrace. He stood at her father's side, his expression bland. But his eyes were like flint.

Fingers frantically tugged at the revealing line of her top—which had become altogether too revealing during her hasty rush out of Howard's arms—and she felt her face grow hot. Ross was following the movement of her shaky hands with icy disgust and that look was all it took to have her back under some sort of control.

She had wanted to make this evening uncomfortable for him, to underline what he must already know—that he was an unwelcome, unwanted intruder into her life. That Howard had played the part assigned to him far too whole-heartedly had to be all to the good. With any luck Ross would decide he didn't want her at any price and would come to some arrangement with her father over the money owing.

Howard was standing now, Ambrose hurriedly introducing him to Ross, and Christa's heart lurched nastily. Ross had an intimidating, thoroughly masculine face—the mouth and the eyes issuing a cool challenge Howard couldn't fail to be aware of. Detestable creature! But he was, she conceded with painful honesty, the most attractive and intriguing man she had ever encountered. Beside him, even Howard's stunning good looks paled into insignificance.

All at once she felt horribly, horribly nervous. Her plans to get back at Ross this evening seemed too childish for words. She hoped against hope that Ross wouldn't detect the way she felt—and then caught his eyes on her, grimly narrowed, the firm mouth set.

Instinctively, she lifted her stubborn chin. She put all her sudden dislike of what she had seen as childish behaviour behind her and thought: Juvenile or not, if my strategy works, I won't be seeing you again. Then she flinched as his silvery gaze wandered insultingly over her body before drifting upwards to meet her affronted eyes with a cruel denigration that shocked the breath out of her lungs.

'Excuse me,' she said thickly, wondering what had happened to her voice. 'I must see to dinner.' And she swept out of the room, fuming. She felt as if he had handled her; her skin crawled with fire. He was loathsome!

'Can I help?'

She was in the kitchen, wildly clattering pans to ease the tension that threatened to pull her into a million chaotic fragments, and as the deep male voice cut through the din she whirled around, her heart thumping, irrationally disappointed to see Howard.

A huge deflating sigh left her lungs, left her feeling weary and unsure of herself. Why had she been so disappointed? she asked herself shakily. Because you'd have liked to rattle these pans around his arrogant head, the answer came back roundly, reassuring her.

'You could take the wine through,' she said, feeling more cheerful now that she had sorted her crazed emotions out.

Two bottles were on the dresser, breathing, cheap but drinkable red wine from the village stores. Howard said, 'Will do,' picking them up and hovering over her as she removed the sizzling pheasants from the oven.

Thankfully, they always had pheasants in the deep-freeze because Ambrose was invited to every shoot around. The vegetables were out of their own garden, she had grown them herself this year, so putting on the style for Ross's benefit wasn't going to cost a bomb.

'You didn't tell me your father's guest was Ross Donahue,' Howard remarked. 'Hell of an interesting man.'

'Is he?' Christa did her best to sound uninterested, wondering what Howard would say if he knew the truth—that her father and Ross were even now probably discussing the details of a forthcoming wedding.

She stifled a groan but Howard was too immersed in his own train of thought to notice.

'He's the first actual multi-millionaire I've ever met. I read an article about him in the *Financial Times* a month or two ago. Apparently, he started work when he was fourteen, and twenty years on he owns a string of highly exclusive restaurants, plus huge hotel complexes all over the world—not to mention his shares in countless others.'

'Nice,' Christa remarked drily, placing the golden-brown pheasants on a hot meat-dish. At least that snippet of information settled something. Any sneaking and unwanted gratitude she might have felt for the way he'd stuck to his word and bailed her father out of deep financial trouble went flying out of the window. He could obviously afford such gestures.

'Nice?' Howard echoed, scoffing. 'Sheer bloody genius, allied to hard graft!' Howard was waxing more enthusiastic with every word he uttered. 'Came up from nothing, actually—you've got to hand it to him—born in a Liverpool slum, one of a huge undisciplined family. That's why he calls his restaurants 'Tinkers'—it seems, when he was growing up, his family were always called that, *'Tinker'* or *'Irish'*. The other slum inhabitants, to quote the article, went out of their way to pour scorn on a family even worse off than they were themselves, socially lower—in the gutter. Fascinating.'

'Fascinating,' Christa echoed slowly, her hands moving sluggishly as she decorated the meat-dish with crisp curls of bacon. Ross had obviously been speaking the truth when he'd said he wanted a wife who would be a social asset, who would open doors previously barred to him. The horrors of his insalubrious childhood, when he and his raggle-taggle family had been considered lower than the gutter his peers inhabited, must still rankle.

Privately, when she had bothered to consider his motives at all, she had wondered at an apparently secure, wealthy, successful man's desire to belong to anything so outmoded and insignificant as the 'county' set. Now it had all been explained, and she knew precisely why she was being used. Curiously, the knowledge hurt, as if, deep in her heart, she had hoped for other, kinder, more flattering motives. But, it seemed, he had been totally honest with her—as she had been with him, she took pains to remind herself. 'I'd make you a rotten wife,' she had said, and so she would—if he still wanted to go through with the whole sick idea at the end of this evening!

Sliding the laden meat-dish into the warming oven, she removed her apron and picked up the tray of chilled salmon mousse.

'All set?' She hoped her smile wasn't too stiff. 'And don't forget—we're hooked on each other, just for this evening. And don't ask why,' she told him as he opened his mouth on a question. 'I'll fill you in some other time.'

When the threat of a forced marriage to Donahue is well and truly over, she promised herself.

'And Howard——' she paused as he held the door open for her '—keep it subtle. Don't overact—you know, keep to adoring glances, the occasional touching of hands, just as we've helped each other out before. Just let the message get through.'

'Who's acting, Chris?' Howard's voice was rough, his eyes assessing, as if he had never seen her before. And that alone should have warned her she was playing with fire. But it didn't—her mind was too full of the detestable Ross Donahue to leave room for anything else.

It had been the worst evening of her life. Oh, the meal had turned out faultlessly; the conversation, on the surface, relaxed. But there had been undercurrents, tensions that made her feel like a tightly coiled spring, every glance from those clever silver eyes making her heart kick.

She hadn't been able properly to respond to Howard's lover-like glances, and when he'd touched her—which seemed to be as often as possible—she had felt annoyed with him, more than anything else. Which had not been the way she'd planned it at all!

And she hadn't planned on feeling sorry for Ross. It seemed absurd to feel any such emotion for a man who so obviously had everything—compelling looks, poise, intelligence, sheer dominating masculine presence and more money than he could possibly know what to do with.

But every time Howard or her father mentioned mutual friends —and many of them were titled, minor, boring aristocracy—she felt a twinge of compassion. Ross might be holding a gun to her head, and she would never forgive him for that, but couldn't he see that when it came to the basics of drive and achievement he was worth more than the whole wretched county set put together?

Her brain in a hopeless jumble, she saw Howard to the door when she realised that she couldn't possibly press him to stay any longer. If someone didn't make a move, she'd thought hysterically, they would still all be sitting round the fire, drinking coffee no one could possibly want, until next Christmas!

Howard took her into his arms in the cool dark hall but she pushed him away. 'Game's over, friend,' she said, resisting the impulse to slap him because the whole farce had been her idea. She was ashamed of that, and didn't know what was wrong with her.

As she heard the Range Rover's engine fire she leaned back against the smooth wood of the door, her eyes closed.

Close to her an incisive voice spoke with quiet warning, 'Don't play games like that again.'

'You startled me!' Christa sucked in an unsteady breath, her eyes widening.

'Good.' He stood directly in front of her, rocking back on his heels. It was difficult to see his face in the dim light, but Christa could imagine the ungiving expression as he promised with silky menace, 'See Howard Mortmain again and I'll do a damn sight more than startle you.'

So the charade with Howard had had the desired effect. But for some unknown reason Christa couldn't feel glad about it. To push her plans further she should be telling him to go to hell, that she would see whom she pleased, when she pleased—before they were married, and after.

But she couldn't do it. Crazily, she wanted to apologise, both for the stupid stunt she had pulled this evening and for the things she'd said to him that night at his flat.

She had said she wouldn't marry him—and that reaction had been predictable, understandable—but, horribly, she'd said she wouldn't touch scum like him with a ten-foot pole, agreed that he was too plebeian...

In the light of what she'd learned of his roots, those taunts had been unforgivable. He might even believe she'd read that article herself, and had said such things precisely because she had!

Christa didn't want him to think that. And perhaps, if she apologised, they could begin again. Try to work some way out of this sorry mess—a way that didn't involve marriage. If she promised to introduce him to the people he mistakenly believed to be his social superiors—made them accept him for the man he was... A genius, Howard had called him...

'Lost for words?' He moved closer. He wasn't touching her but she felt crowded, smothered by the searing challenge of his potent masculinity. It made her feel threatened, unable to cope, weak with a fear she couldn't put a name to.

Knowing she had to reach a new understanding with him, but not quite sure how to go about it, she began huskily, hoping he would see the sense of her offered introductions, without the need for a loveless marriage, 'Can't we talk about this——' only to be cut short with brutal thoroughness.

'I've said all I intend to say on the subject of Mortmain, and as for talking—that was the purpose of this evening's visit. However, you chose to hide behind that guy and it's too damned late now. Somewhere between the third and the fourth cup of coffee I lost what little patience I had left.'

He moved past her, opening the door, admitting a blast of cool night air. 'I have just one instruction—give in your notice on Monday morning. You won't be working after we're married because we will be out of the country as much as we're in it. And if you need to discuss details of our wedding, talk to your father. I've told him precisely what I have in mind. See you at the altar.'

And that was a threat, if ever she'd heard one. She stood staring at the closed door for long minutes after she'd heard him drive away, anger rebuilding inside her, brick by solid brick, stronger than ever before.

She had actually wanted to apologise to him, try to work something out—something beneficial to both of them. But he, in his typically high-handed way, had refused to let her get a word in. Did he think he could treat her that way, like a mindless doll? Did he think he could pull her life to pieces around her and get away with it?

She would see him in hell before she made any such overture to him again. From here on in it was war. Married to him or not, it was war!

CHAPTER SIX

CHRISTA struggled to fasten the tiny buttons on the back of her wedding dress and found, predictably, that the task was beyond her. She wasn't a contortionist so, her face set, she opened her bedroom door and called her father.

He appeared almost immediately, looking so elegant in a beautifully tailored morning suit that, at first, she hardly recognised him. No doubt Ross had paid for his gear, as he had paid for hers, she decided with a *frisson* of distaste.

She hadn't seen Ross since the night of the dreadful dinner party three weeks ago, but out of sight hadn't been out of mind. Almost daily something had happened to remind her that he was to play an important part in her life—the most important part, she conceded regretfully.

Workmen had arrived to wrench the broad expanses of rough grass back to their former smooth emerald-green lawn status and when, bemused by the activity, she had asked her father what was going on he had told her.

She and Ross were to be married in the ancient estate church and the reception would be held in a huge marquee on the lawn—hence the continual rolling and mowing. And within no time at all the tiny church had been opened up, cleaned and polished until it looked as if it had never been closed at all. Lawns had emerged from the unkempt grass, the borders cleared of weeds, and tubs of hydrangeas and lilies had been sunk into the ground to hide the gaps left by the herbaceous plants that had succumbed to disease and neglect.

Christa had accepted the transformations philosophically; merely reflecting, somewhat acidly, that it was wonderful to see what a fat bank account allied to steely determination could do. But when the more personal items had begun to arrive she had felt quite differently.

It was one thing for him to pay enormous sums to have the grounds smartened up. It would be his wedding, too, and if he felt the need to have a huge, distinguished guest list drawn mainly from the ranks of her father's county friends—to make an impression—then that was his affair. But did he have to thrust his arbitrary nose into her concerns?

The wedding dress, the matching silk-covered shoes, the dainty lingerie, lay untouched in their elegant boxes after delivery. It had been as much as she could do to even think about them, let alone take them from the layers of tissue paper and handle them.

But this morning, reluctantly and of necessity, she had stepped into the miracle of heavy oyster silk, half hoping it wouldn't fit, more than half inclined to walk up the aisle in her gardening gear just to give him a foretaste of what he was letting himself in for.

However, as she might have known, the gown fitted perfectly, or would do when the dozens of tiny buttons had been fitted into the corresponding holes, and she had too much pride to present herself before the wedding guests looking like a tramp. She would not make such a public statement of her discontent. Her hateful marriage to Ross would be a private thing.

Her father was blowing out his cheeks as he stooped to do up the buttons and Christa stared at her reflection in the mirror with stormy eyes. The fitted dress gave her slender figure a flattering emphasis before swirling away in soft folds from her hips, the inserted flaring panels of matching lace adding elegance, mystery.

Silently, she handed her mother's pearls to Ambrose and she could feel the way his hands shook as he dealt with the intricate fastener.

His face, reflected over her shoulder, was as pale as hers, and she met his eyes, not knowing what to say, not knowing if there was anything left to say.

'It's been emotional blackmail, hasn't it, Christa?' he murmured heavily. He looked as if he didn't like himself, or the world he found himself in. 'All these weeks and you haven't said a word, haven't blamed me.'

'It can't be undone,' she replied tautly, knowing that if she softened by the merest fraction she would burst into tears. Clenching her teeth, she reached up to tease a few curling strands of hair from the smooth upswept style she had decided on when the circular coronet of fresh orange-blossom that was to secure her veil had arrived earlier.

'But it can.' Her father's eyes, when she met them in the glass, were anguished. 'It's not too late. Call it off. I'll face the music—I want you to know that.'

'Call it off?' she echoed, her eyes widening as she swung round to face him. '*You'd* advise me to do that!'

'Yes.' His face was white, his hands shaking, but he looked very determined. 'I've come out of this affair badly, I know that. I'm not proud of myself. My only excuse is that I thought you'd be happy with Donahue. He's a decent chap, brainy, a sticker. He's got style, as well as looks and money. Integrity. Married to him, you'd never want for a single thing, and I told myself he'd make you happy, that love would grow. But seeing you with Howard started me thinking. I didn't think you and he were anything other than good friends. But if you're in love with him, Christa, or even if you only think you could be, then call this wedding off.'

'I'm not in love with Howard,' Christa replied drearily. She didn't want her father to carry a heavier burden than the one he already shouldered so she had to tell him the truth.

Besides, Donahue had paid her father's debts and the price of that had been her agreement to this wedding. She had accepted her part in this horrible farce and she wasn't backing down.

'The whole thing with Howard was a put-up job,' she confessed, reaching for the fine lace veil, securing the fragrant coronet with steady fingers. 'Howard and I staged the lovey-dovey act to rub Ross up the wrong way.'

It had seemed a rational idea at the time but precisely how irrational it had been was reflected in her father's quick, worried statement,

'Don't ever do anything like that again. He'd be a dangerous man to fool around with. You'd be the loser, Christa.'

Loser or not, she heard the sibilant murmur of approval as she walked down the aisle on her father's arm, the luxurious fabric of her gown swaying elegantly around her long, slender legs. She didn't look at Ross. Throughout the ceremony she kept her head high, and the delicate spray of freesias and orange blossoms she held was perfectly steady, betraying not the slightest sign of nerves.

Only Christa knew that her heart was fluttering like a trapped wild thing, that every pore of her skin seemed to tingle with a painful awareness of the man at her side.

Only by exercising iron control could she get through this ceremony at all.

When Ross gently lifted her veil she knew they were man and wife. She had murmured her responses automatically, hardly aware of what she was doing, and as she caught the silver gleam of his eyes, the slight softening of the hard male mouth as he lowered his head, waves of icy shock engulfed her. She thought, this can't be happening, but she knew it was, and her lips were icy beneath his, stiff, as her whole body rejected the warmth of his mouth.

As if in a dream, she watched herself leave the church on her husband's arm, heard the hubbub of congratulations, the clicks of cameras. She barely noticed the short drive home in a chauffeur-driven limo hired for the occasion, the marquee—sumptuously decorated with what seemed like a million flowers—and the food, the champagne, of the very best.

Even the weather was perfect. And beneath the clear blue skies she saw herself and Ross as others would see them, a perfect couple. She, so slender and fair, almost ethereal in her soft silk gown with flowers circling her elegant head. He, the perfect foil, a tall, dark, perfectly proportioned male. And the way he never strayed an inch from her side, protective, lover-like—no onlooker would be able to fault the groom's tender behaviour towards his new bride.

'Christa—my dear—how very lovely you look! My heartiest congratulations to you both!' Lady Maude, Howard's great-aunt, teetered forward on tiny feet, her flower-decked hat askew.

'Thank you.' Ross's smile was urbane, as if he met slightly batty titled ladies every day of his life and knew exactly how to deal with them. But Christa saw the glitter of satisfaction in those silver eyes and thought, Creep! Though she pinned a smile to her face, for Lady Maude's benefit, because she had always liked the eccentric old thing and was sorry for her, too. She lived alone now, rattling round in a barn of a mansion, and when her loneliness got too much for her to bear she cajoled her elderly servants into action and threw a lavish dinner party, inviting half the county.

Ross was charming the old lady, Christa noted without surprise, hanging on her every word. Now Lady Maude tipped her amazingly decorated head on one side and said archly, '*So* nice to have a new addition to our circle. One meets so few fresh, *interesting* faces these days. Ambrose tells me you and Christa are to make your home at the Hall. Splendid!' A heavily ringed hand swooped out to relieve a passing waiter of one of the glasses on his tray and Ross deftly caught the empty champagne glass she had automatically loosed when a full one became available. 'You must both come to my birthday party in September,' Lady Maude invited gaily, half emptying her fresh glass. 'It may very well be my last— I'm not getting younger—so I shall invite simply *everyone* in the hope of receiving a great many presents!'

'You've been saying that for the last ten years at least,' Christa grinned. 'And you'll still be saying it ten years hence. You're an old fraud!'

'I know. I'm incorrigible, or so I'm told!' The old lady's eyes twinkled over the rim of her glass, plainly relishing Ross's appreciative smile. 'But do say you'll come.'

'We'd be absolutely delighted,' Ross said warmly, his voice a velvet purr, and Christa thought, He's never spoken to me like that, in that tone, or smiled at me that way, as if I were the only woman in the world.

It was a strangely bitter thought, and one she was at a loss to understand. She didn't want Ross to sweet-talk her, heaven forbid! And she couldn't possibly be jealous of dear old Lady Maude!

Nevertheless, it was a relief to see Howard easing his way through a crowd of guests, his handsome face wry. Christa smiled spontaneously, moving forward to meet him. She knew what must have happened, having witnessed several similar occasions in the past—he had been despatched by his father to take his great-aunt in hand. She became notoriously outrageous after a few glasses of wine and Howard was her favourite relative and best able to handle her.

But if she'd thought Ross was too engrossed with Lady Maude to notice she'd moved away from his side, she was mistaken. A firm hand caught her by her waist in a no-nonsense grip that hauled her back to him, crushing her against his hard lean length.

Through the fine silk of her dress she could feel the sheer power of his potent male body, feel his warmth. This contact was like a consummation in itself, shattering her with a total awareness of him as a man. And she alone recognised the threat as he said suavely, 'Christa and I should be getting changed—I'm running a tight schedule.' To Lady Maude, and to Howard, who had reached them by now and had a steadying hand on his great-aunt's arm, it would sound like an impatient bridegroom's excuse to be alone with his bride, and he compounded this impression by adding, huskily, to Christa, 'We have a busy time ahead of us, my darling.'

And then his mouth took hers, as if he couldn't wait a moment longer to take her in his arms, to taste her lips.

Shocked to complete immobility, Christa couldn't draw away and make a lightly teasing joke of her groom's unexpected and far too public display of passion. And, as her total awareness became concentrated on the tantalising pressure of his mouth on hers, she found she didn't want to draw away.

Unheeding of their audience, her body melted into his, and as if she had no control over her actions she felt the dominating breadth of his shoulders as her arms moved to hold him.

Shatteringly, a giddying sensation of need engulfed her, a primitive yearning need that the kisses she'd exchanged with one or two other men in the past had in no way prepared her for. She didn't know how to begin to cope—didn't even think she really wanted to cope—with the delicious and utterly new sensations that were creating havoc as, sensing her receptive response, the pressure of his lips altered, becoming more erotic, deeper, completely proprietorial. She could have stayed in his arms forever, like this, savouring him, drowning in the bone-melting nearness of him...

'We really should make a move.' Shockingly, he was the one to break the kiss; to move slightly away, his voice damningly cool, his eyes mocking, knowing.

He hadn't felt a thing, Christa realised, her hand going to her breast as if to quieten the frantic beating of her heart.

Horribly, she felt herself blush, and it wasn't due to the affectionate amusement in the eyes of the guests who had been close enough to witness the staged scene. It was because she had seen the shuttered look on Howard's face. Because that scene had been staged—she only had to glance from Howard's tight features to the grim line of satisfaction stamped on Ross's sensual mouth to know that. Ross had used her, had used that kiss to stamp his authority in front of Howard.

Tit for tat, she acknowledged with a ragged sigh. And Howard was looking more upset than he had any right to be. Apart from which, having gained her equilibrium, she was hopping mad—mainly with herself.

To Ross, that kiss had been an exercise in one-upmanship, nothing more. Ross wasn't interested in her as a woman, only as a wife who would open doors for him previously closed. But she, dammit, had responded. He couldn't have failed to notice her eagerness—it had given him the edge over her, and that she definitely didn't want. Foolishly, she had actually enjoyed being kissed by him—had welcomed the strange feeling of rightness, of belonging in his arms. So kissing him back had been a dangerous exercise and one she would make sure she didn't repeat!

'We'll only be here for one night, so make the most of it.'

Christa stared round the honeymoon suite in the superb hotel on the Rue d'Astor, her eyes stormy. He had hardly exchanged a dozen words with her since they had left the reception and now, newly installed in one of the most luxurious hotels Paris had to offer, she wasn't in the mood for chit-chat.

'Where then?' she asked tersely, glaring at the huge canopied bed with acute distaste.

The only clue to the honeymoon destination had come from her father a couple of weeks ago when he had asked if her passport was in order. She didn't care where they went—the whole idea of a honeymoon in their circumstances was ludicrous, anyway—but it would be nice to have some idea!

'Cannes. We'll be staying at my villa for a couple of weeks.' He was already loosening his tie and Christa looked quickly away. After the reception he had changed into a dark three-piece suit with a very faint charcoal pinstripe. He looked more like a man about to embark on a heavy business meeting rather than on a honeymoon. But then, she reminded herself tartly, this was no ordinary honeymoon.

He had removed his jacket now, hanging it in one of the king-sized wardrobes, and Christa turned her back on him, walking slowly over the sumptuous carpet, an idle hand trailing over surfaces, fabrics. She was disgustingly nervous and trying not to let it show. She had reached one of the windows when his voice hit her, making her spine go rigid with tension.

'I'm taking a shower now, how about joining me?' It was huskily said, a wealth of invitation in the tone, and Christa's cheeks went pink, her hands bunching into fists at her sides as she bit out, 'Thanks, but no thanks.' She might have responded to that kiss with more enthusiasm than was wise, and he would have had to have been an idiot not to know it. But he needn't think she would be willing to repeat the performance, or to allow him the liberties he obviously thought he was entitled to!

'I rather thought not.' He didn't sound disappointed, far from it. A soft tuneful whistle accompanied the rustle of clothing and Christa stared out of the window, her fixed gaze absorbing nothing at all, tension coiling inside her like a spring. And, like a spring, she twirled round as soon as she heard the bathroom door close, the hiss of the shower.

Apart from the voluptuous bed, the room contained wildly expensive Empire-style furniture, too ornate for her taste, and a pretty but uncomfortable-looking sofa against one wall. It would do at a pinch, if nothing else offered, she decided, hurrying through the open double doors that led to the suite's private sitting room.

Small Empire chairs, very elegant and not terribly functional, were placed around a couple of low tables, and there was a dining table and two upright chairs in a window alcove.

It would have to be the sofa, she acknowledged regretfully. She would have preferred him to sleep in an entirely separate room, but not even she could be optimistic enough to expect him to agree to spend the night on one of those small stiff chairs.

Grabbing the heavily embroidered slippery satin quilt from the bed, plus one of the satin-covered pillows, she piled them on the sofa. His indifference in the face of her refusal to join him in the shower hadn't fooled her.

He wasn't a man who gave way easily to physical desire—he had proved that much to her when he had shown himself to be completely unmoved by the passionate embrace he had staged at the reception.

He would always be in control of himself, of any situation. His upbringing, his fight to climb out of the slums to the very pinnacle of his chosen business sphere, would have made him chary of showing his emotions to anyone or allowing them to get out of control, to rule him.

But that didn't mean he didn't have a normal man's needs and desires—he probably had more of those than was good for him, she decided grimly. With those compelling looks, that healthy physique, he would have no trouble finding willing female partners with whom to slake those physical needs. So he probably thought he would be able to take her like plucking a ripe plum from a tree—whenever he wanted to. And her unthinking response to his kiss would have firmly reinforced that belief.

Well, he was in for one big surprise!

But he sounded more amused than surprised when he came through from the bathroom, a towel slung precariously around his narrow hips, his hair rough-dried and appealingly ruffled, droplets of water still clinging to his body hair.

'Decided we'd be too warm in bed with that quilt?' he enquired silkily, his mouth quirking. 'Aren't you being rather premature?'

She didn't know what he meant by that, and wasn't going to ask. She wished he'd put some clothes on and stop looking at her as if he found her *funny*. The silvery eyes, thickly fringed with black, held a definite gleam of amusement which she didn't like at all.

'I wouldn't like you to be cold on the sofa,' she explained haughtily, tearing her eyes away from the intriguing dusting of dark hair that disappeared beneath the edge of the low-slung towel around his hips.

'Such wifely concern,' he countered sardonically. 'I have no intention of sleeping on the sofa.'

'Then I will!' Cheeks flaming with annoyance, she grabbed her flight bag and stamped to the bathroom, slamming the door behind her. He had forced her to marry him, but he couldn't force her to share his bed. Not tonight, not *ever*.

But sheer temper wasn't going to achieve anything, she decided when she at last stepped from beneath the shower, considerably chastened by the direction her thoughts had taken her. This was the first day of their marriage. She and Ross had a long way to go before it could end in divorce. So it would make sense to forget the rage and to approach the situation calmly and directly, to lay down the ground rules.

She towelled herself dry, pondering. They couldn't spend the whole of their time together bickering and sniping; it would be too tiresome for words.

If they had talked things through before their marriage they could have reached an understanding by now. But, for reasons best known to himself, Ross had kept well away from her during their short, farcical engagement. That she had adroitly side-stepped his intention to discuss their future—using Howard as a shield to hide behind—was something she wasn't too proud of now.

Quickly, she rummaged in her flight bag for the nightdress she had bundled in along with her toiletries. Experiencing a fleeting regret for the satin and lace confections Ross had had delivered to the Hall, she dragged the demure cotton gown over her head. She had been right to leave those expensive pieces of nonsense behind, she told herself staunchly. She didn't want anything of his.

Dragging her shower cap off, she pushed her fingers through the tumbled, silver-gilt mane of her hair and left the bathroom in search of her unwanted husband.

He was in the doorway between the bedroom and the sitting-room and it looked as if he had been waiting for her. He was wearing a white thigh-length towelling robe that accentuated the darkness of his skin tones, and made him look incredibly sexy.

'Would you like some supper, something to drink?' He tossed back the remainder of the scotch in his glass and Christa watched the ripple of his throat and felt her own close up.

'No, thanks.' She refused both offers with husky difficulty, edging closer to the sofa, feeling definitely skittery. Suddenly her plain cotton nightdress seemed to offer no protection at all. He was looking at her as if he could see right through it to the over-warm, apprehensively tingling flesh beneath.

A trickle of sensation shivered down her spine as she realised that he was capable of arousing her without even touching her. If she didn't know it had actually happened she wouldn't have believed any man capable of doing such a thing to her! She was off balance. She didn't even like him, she didn't really know him—so how could he possibly have this effect on her?

All thoughts of having a calm rational discussion about their future fled her brain, leaving it empty and horribly receptive to the effect of his intent assessment of her. His intimidatingly masculine presence filled the room, insinuating itself into her very pores, making logical thought impossible.

'I'm tired,' she muttered defensively, mentally postponing all thoughts of a serious discussion until the morning. Her mouth dropped open in shock as he moved closer, close enough for her to recognise the warm glitter in his eyes as sexual interest.

'It has been a hectic day,' he agreed smokily, the softening curve of his mouth letting her know that sleep was the last thing on his mind. And just looking at his mouth made her remember precisely how she had felt when he'd kissed her that morning—remember, too, the reason behind that seemingly passionate embrace.

And that was enough to have her hauling herself together. Hurriedly, she snatched the quilt she'd put ready on the sofa and wrapped it around her, her fingers clumsy. She was through being used, and she told him so, her chin jutting defiantly. 'We sleep in separate beds. Separate rooms in future, preferably. And if that doesn't tie in with your ideas of marriage—tough! I'm already earning my keep. Lady Maude's wasn't the only invitation we'll get. You'll soon find yourself invited to more social thrashes than even you can handle.'

It was as if she'd poured a bucket of icy water over him, she realised as she sank down on the sofa, the quilt pulled up to her chin. He seemed to freeze, something cold looking out of his eyes.

'My willing bride,' he snapped sarcastically, silver eyes darkening as they swept over her, deriding the way she was cowering behind the quilt.

And what *did* he expect? Christa thought explosively—that she would meekly allow him to make the ultimate use of her body?

'Willing!' she snorted, violet eyes glinting. 'I've first-hand knowledge of what life can be with a gambling addict. Do you think I'd *willingly* be married to just such another?'

'I've already told you,' he said with forced patience, 'I don't gamble.' He stood over her, a stern implacable figure, and Christa almost regretted the loss of the warm, slightly teasing, sexually aware man who had been with her in this room only a few moments ago. 'I went to Lassiter's that night because I had reason to believe that one of my chefs was there. Pierre is brilliant at his job, but he gambles. When I hired him I knew his past record but I opted to give him a chance to prove himself. But about twelve months ago he went completely off the rails and I had to bail him out of trouble. I gave him one last chance, told him that the next time he lapsed he'd lose his job. This time he'd been missing for days, and Alec Canfield had phoned his lodgings but had got no response. Then he had an anonymous phone call—as it turned out, it had come from the under-chef who had been filling in for him, and was based on petty professional rivalry. The caller said that Pierre had been practically living at Lassiter's, gambling heavily.

'I was just back from the States and pretty disgusted by what I saw then as Pierre's disloyalty, his damned stupidity. I went with the intention of dragging him away, and found your father instead.' He shot her a look of hard distaste. 'Pierre, as I later discovered, had come down with flu. He'd been feeling too ill to make the effort to phone in to Alec, too ill to answer the phone when it rang.'

He swung round on his heel, saying distantly, 'I need another drink,' and then, more softly, 'You'll be stiff as a board if you insist on sleeping on that. Get into bed—I won't touch you if you don't want me to.'

Was that meant to reassure her? If so, it didn't work! Violet eyes stabbed the back of his wide shoulders as he disappeared into the sitting-room, then she wriggled further beneath the quilt and firmly closed her eyes. She was not sharing a bed with him, and that was that! He would get precisely what he had married her for—social acceptance—and not a single thing more.

Righteous indignation kept her awake until, some time later, she heard him get into bed. And then, in the darkness, she found herself wondering what made him tick. Up until now she had thought of him as nothing more than a ruthless social climber, trampling smaller weaker people beneath his feet without a single qualm. But somehow that didn't tie in with the picture of a highly successful man taking the trouble to give a known gambler a second chance, who cared enough about what

he had believed to be a straying employee to go himself
to drag him out of Lassiter's clutches.

And later something else, something she couldn't put
a name to, kept her tossing and turning on the hard sofa,
her body burning almost feverishly as her sensitised ears
picked up every sound, every even sleeping breath he
took, each rustle of the bedcovers as he turned languidly
in his effortless slumbers.

CHAPTER SEVEN

NOTHING had prepared Christa for Cannes. The sheer beauty of the bay, La Croisette, the chic hotels and restaurants, the sparkling busy harbour where luxurious yachts lazily bobbed at anchor, dwarfed by the magnificent Alpes Maritimes, rendered her speechless with unwilling appreciation as Ross negotiated the hired Citroën on to the Rue d'Antibes where sophisticated shops offered merchandise to tempt even the most frugal-minded.

If this had been a normal honeymoon, and if she and the remote-faced man at her side had been deeply in love instead of strangers brought together by the ugly combination of financial and social need, then she would have been feeling ecstatic. As it was, she merely grunted when eventually Ross pulled on to a paved forecourt in front of a white stone villa and told her, 'I bought it as my Cote d'Azur base several years ago—I have half a dozen restaurants in this area, plus shares in several hotels. And although we'll make Liddiat Hall our permanent home, I want you to look on the villa as yours. We'll come here to relax whenever you wish.'

The engine stopped, he had turned in his seat, his eyes on her. Today he had chosen to wear light-coloured cotton trousers, and a casual designer shirt in a deep blue that introduced aquamarine flecks to those silvery eyes.

A sideways glance showed a softening in those harshly drawn near-perfect features. The thick, almost black hair was expensively cut yet attractively unsubdued, hinting at an untamed individuality which, annoyingly, appealed to her strongly and went way beyond mere male good looks.

Christa stared stiffly ahead, her mind working uncomfortably, wondering if he expected a gush of gratitude, a simper or two. She decided he didn't. Such artificial posings would hardly please him. He no doubt expected a normal show of interest, but even that was beyond her. They wouldn't be married long enough for her to take advantage of his offer, appealing though it might be.

'Still sulking?' he enquired with a purring menace that spoke of patience nearing its limits. 'I shall have to see what I can do about that.' A finger trailed idly over the delicate contours of her cheek, from the small hollow of her temple to the soft curve of her mouth, and Christa flinched as though stung, her skin on fire where he had touched it.

Her heart pumping, she scrambled out of the car, the fierce midday heat burning through her cotton T-shirt. His face was grim, she noted, willing her pulse-rate to settle back down to normal. But if he thought her reaction was disgust at his touch then that was all to the good. Only she knew the truth—that his very nearness, never mind his touch, upset her equilibrium to such an extent that she hardly knew where she was, or who she was! His sheer physical magnetism threatened to overwhelm her, and that wasn't what she wanted at all!

But the rigid line of his shoulders, as he lifted their luggage from the boot, relaxed as a pleased, 'Ross— welcome home!' cut through the silence.

'Sabine!' The grim features lightened and Christa glanced towards the villa where a skinny middle-aged woman came down the white stone steps.

'You had a good journey, yes?' A smile of pure welcome irradiated the plain features. 'Since your phone call I have made everything ready for you and Madame Donahue.' The lightly accented voice was charming but the shrewd dark eyes were definitely cool as they rested assessingly on Christa.

'Darling, meet Sabine, who looks after the villa for me,' Ross introduced, smiling as the Frenchwoman reluctantly held out her hand.

There was more than a hint of reserve in the housekeeper's manner towards her, Christa decided, but there was no mistaking the other woman's admiration for her employer or the sincerity of her welcome as she told him, 'It is so good to see you again, Ross. It has been too long. And I have made the big room ready, but if I have forgotten anything you will tell me, yes?'

Sabine bent to pick up the heavy suitcases, but Ross took them from her, stopping her protests with a grin.

'Run along and put the kettle on. I think my wife could use a cup of tea.'

'But of course.' All the Frenchwoman's pleasure drained from her dark eyes as they turned coldly to Christa, her voice ever so slightly denigrating as she added, 'Such a very English habit.' She made the remark sound vaguely insulting and Christa gave a mental shrug. So the housekeeper didn't like her; she had apparently been judged and found wanting within the space of a few minutes. She probably thought, quite wrongly, that she, Christa, would start throwing her weight around, upset the obviously cosy relationship she had with her employer. It was annoying, but she could live with it, and she unwillingly followed Ross as he carried the cases up the steps.

The interior of the villa was cool and airy, the stone floors and the fresh white walls enriched by soft rugs and beautiful tapestries, the tasteful placement of lovingly polished dark wood furniture and lush green plants in carved marble urns.

Christa felt distinctly out of place—her light denim jeans and very ordinary T-shirt didn't blend with the style and elegance of her surroundings. She half regretted the sheer perversity that had led her to dress in the first things she'd pulled out of her haphazardly packed suitcase this morning. But she had been feeling out of sorts, she excused herself. Her night had been virtually sleepless, and the reason for that was something she didn't want to think about.

At the head of the curving stone stairs Ross stopped abruptly outside an open door.

'Sabine will be disappointed,' he remarked, his voice carefully level. 'But no matter—since you insist on separate beds.'

Glancing over his shoulder, Christa took in the huge shadowy room, a massive four-poster bed taking pride of place, great urns and bowls of cut flowers bathing the room with their sweet, provocative scent.

So that was the 'big room' Sabine had referred to, Christa thought, trudging down the thickly carpeted corridor in Ross's wake, and hovering in the doorway of a smaller, much less flamboyant room where he had already disposed the suitcases, one at the end of each narrow twin bed.

'You may as well come inside,' he remarked drily, crossing to the huge window to raise the blinds, admitting golden sunlight. Beyond him, through the window, Christa saw the view of La Croisette and caught her breath, her heart lifting with pleasure.

It would be nice to set their undoubted difficulties aside for just one moment, to tell him how beautiful she found his home, she thought, but she was forestalled by his impatient, 'I don't know how the hell I'm going to explain this to Sabine. She obviously went to a great deal of trouble to get the master suite ready for us. I neglected to tell her that my wife refuses to share a bed with me.'

'Does it matter what the housekeeper thinks?' Christa snapped, furious because he had effectively ruined the one pleasant moment they could have shared, though why that should bother her, let alone make her hopping mad, she couldn't imagine.

'Of course it matters.' His eyes were hard as he turned to face her. 'And Sabine isn't a housekeeper, or certainly not in the sense you mean—a lowly *servant*,' he stressed the word insultingly, 'beneath the notice or consideration of someone like you.' After grating out that insult he went on more levelly, 'I need someone to look after the villa and she does it more out of affection for me than a need for the wages she receives. She has feelings, too, and will think that her efforts haven't pleased us. But you wouldn't understand that, would you?' His voice flayed her again, his mouth curling derisively. 'You've never had to earn your own living—you just idled around at home with Daddy, never doing a hand's turn, I don't doubt, until you were forced to when there was no money left to pay for help.'

'Then *you* go and sleep in that glorified flower bower!' Christa yelped. She hated him. Oh, how she hated him! Without knowing a single thing about her he had decided she was an unmitigated snob, uncaring, idle, selfish! But she wasn't about to put him right, tell him that when she had lived at home, during her schooldays, before she'd left to make a life for herself, a career, she had worked as hard, if not harder, than the people her father had then been able to employ.

'I told you I wanted a separate room,' she added tersely, ignoring the dangerous glints in his eyes. 'I will sleep here—you please yourself which bedroom you use, so long as it's not this one!'

'So defensive,' he mocked, his mouth cruel, and he moved towards her. Christa backed away, her mouth dry, and would have gone on backing until she fell right out of the window, but Sabine poked her head round the door and her expression would have been laughable had Christa been in the mood to find anything amusing.

'So—I came to find you to say that tea is waiting by the pool. But you are not there. You are here?'

'We've decided to use this room,' Ross explained with an apparent lightness, then launched into a torrent of rapid French that left Christa standing and had Sabine smiling grimly.

'The English! *Mad!* Tea is by the pool, do not let that spoil also!'

An indulgent smile softened Ross's face as he watched Sabine leave and something hard and hot and painful lodged itself in Christa's breast. What had he told Sabine, to make her smile that way? That he and Madame Donahue didn't sleep together? That the last thing either of them wanted to do was to cavort around in that big luxurious bed?

It was the truth, heaven knew it was, so why did she suddenly and quite violently object to its being broadcast?

Unable to stop herself, she demanded thickly, 'What did you say to her?' and planted her hands on her hips, her lower lip mutinous. She didn't like being laughed at, at least not by the woman who had looked at her with such barely concealed dislike. And she didn't like the way her husband had spoken to Sabine in French, too rapidly for her to be able to follow it, smiling, as if he and his doting housekeeper shared a very private joke.

Her husband! Somehow that thought had got mixed up with the snappy remark she had intended to make next—it left her floundering, and into the silence Ross drawled with amusement,

'I merely explained that being cold-blooded—coming as you do from a notoriously cool and rainy climate—you would find it too hot to actually sleep in a bed with me, the nights here being decidedly warm at this time of year. Now, shall we go and get that tea? Sabine was right, it will spoil if we leave it any longer.'

He reached out and took her hand, drawing her with him out of the room, but she didn't want the contact. Touching him disturbed her. And more angry with her reaction to him than with him, she dragged her fingers out of his grasp.

'I don't have to be led like a child,' she snapped, and he gave a low grunt of laughter.

'Then don't behave like one.'

Scowling at his retreating back, she followed. She didn't trust his unwarranted good humour. He was behaving as if he knew something she didn't, something that gratified him and changed the accent of their uncomfortable relationship. And because she was still mad at him for telling Sabine that she, Christa, was cold-blooded—implying that she was a pallid wimp without enough good red blood to endure the sexual heat of sharing his bed—she drawled nastily, 'I meant what I said. We sleep in separate rooms,' and was further infuriated when he merely lifted his wide shoulders in an uncaring shrug.

*   *   *

The large pool area was paved, surrounded by a walled garden that was neatly laid out in formal parterres with tiny lavender hedges and raked gravel paths.

The tea, with small tomato and chive sandwiches and tiny iced cakes, had been welcome and delicious and even her muddled and tense emotions hadn't dulled her appetite until Ross stood up, stretching.

'I'm going to have a swim. Join me?'

Christa tried to look away and couldn't. His stretching movement had erotically tightened the fabric of his shirt and trousers, accentuating that powerful, all-male physique. He had a beautiful body, not overly muscular but packed with whippy power, perfectly proportioned, with the economical litheness of a superb male animal.

Gulping, she managed at last to tear her eyes away and fixed them on her short transluscent fingernails, studying them with singular attention as she murmured, 'You go ahead. I didn't bring a swimsuit.'

'No hassle,' he told her casually, already walking back to the villa. 'I'll ask Sabine to find something for you.'

'But I don't want...' she began, then subsided back in her chair with a deep sigh. He had already passed through the open glass doors, not bothering, as usual, to listen to what she said, to take her reactions into account. But disregarding her opinions was the story of their short and impossible relationship, she acceded grumpily.

Squeezing herself another cup of tea from the pot, she sipped it thoughtfully. She had decided, only yesterday, that they had to get their relationship on to a more tolerable footing. She could partly understand his need to be accepted socially, given his awful childhood. That it was, in her opinion, a mistaken ambition didn't make it less valid. It was possibly the only ambition left to him, she decided.

His faith in himself, his astute business acumen—coupled with his powerful personality and fantastic looks—had already given him everything a man could want. So being accepted by the kind of people who would have been appalled by the conditions surrounding his early years was the only need he had to fulfil.

So, she would promise to get him invitations and introductions to the cream of society occasions and personages—here her nose wrinkled at his misguided notions—and appear in public at his side, giving every indication that they were a united and devoted couple, if he would agree to a divorce in, say, a couple of years' time. That should give him long enough to get this bug out of his system and to understand that the so-called 'county' set was nothing special.

And that meant that, starting from now, she would have to be more accommodating, not yell at him for the least little thing, learn to bite her tongue a little. Her original intention had been to make life hell for him, to present him with the poisonous wife she had threatened to be. But, for some odd reason, that plan no longer held any appeal.

She had to start somewhere, and joining him in the pool was as good a place as any. Besides, the afternoon was hot and clear blue water very inviting...

The lemon-yellow one piece swimsuit Sabine had brought to the poolside fitted perfectly, Christa decided, appraising her reflection in the full-length mirror on the wall of the set of changing rooms adjacent to the pool area. The cut-away sides made her legs look endless, and if more of her breasts was on view than she thought strictly decent—what did it matter?

Ross had demonstrated very clearly that, sexually, he could take her or leave her. The only time he had made any physical advance to her at all had been when he'd kissed her at the reception. And that had been solely for Howard's benefit, to stamp his mark of ownership in front of the younger man. The embrace had left him totally unmoved.

True, he had invited her to join him in the shower last night, to share his bed. But when she'd refused he had acted as if he had expected as much, and he certainly hadn't seemed to mind one way or the other. Which was, in a way she couldn't quite understand, pretty galling. He was masculine—very—male sexuality seeming to ooze out of his pores, and she had no doubt that if she showed willing he would take whatever was on offer and count it a bonus.

But that wasn't for her—thanks all the same! Her own shaming arousal at his slightest touch—even the touch of those glinting silver eyes—was enough to tell her that, given the right circumstances, she would succumb to his undoubted expertise with an abandonment hitherto quite foreign to her.

She had never been promiscuous; the few men she had dated hadn't had the power to arouse her. Enjoying a goodnight kiss, the companionable warmth of a man's arm around her shoulders, had been as far as it had gone for her. But now, her feminine instincts warned her, she could quite easily become shamelessly wanton in the arms of her husband.

That he was her husband made no difference at all. Sex without love was empty, squalid, and she didn't love him, she didn't even like him. He had forced her into marriage for the most dubious, snobbish reasons, and she would never forgive him for that.

But she had to make a token show of acceptance, she admitted ruefully as she twisted her hair on top of her head and secured it with the lemon-yellow bandeau Sabine had provided. Because, viewed calmly, marriage, even if it was in name only, would quickly become insupportable if it were a constant battleground.

He was already in the pool when she walked from the changing rooms. And far from showing off a racing crawl, which was what she would have expected his macho persona to produce, he was peacefully floating on his back, his eyes closed in sensuous enjoyment of the cool silky water, the warmth of the sun.

Oddly, his total relaxation, his supreme indifference to her presence, enraged her more than any amount of overt male interest would have done. Using the low springboard, she dived cleanly into the water, the ensuing commotion of waves rocking him. And as she set off down the length of the pool in a crawl which compensated in style for what it lacked in speed, she was pleased to see him haul himself out of the water. She had as effectively ruined his physical relaxation as he had ruined her emotional peace and that was a satisfaction—of sorts.

At last, when protesting muscles and lungs could endure no more punishment, Christa pulled herself over the side. Ross was relaxing on one of the loungers, reading, his tanned body daunting, dangerous, even in repose. She began to walk towards him, nervous butterflies lurching around in her stomach.

She knew she looked good, that every detail of her body was on view beneath the thin, clinging wet fabric of her borrowed swimsuit. She also knew that she had never been so vividly aware of herself as a woman.

Almost lazily, she reached up and removed the bandeau, shaking her head so that the bright mane of her hair flew this way and that before settling riotously around her shoulders. And Ross looked up and, meeting the coolness of his silver eyes she felt warmth spread through the lower part of her stomach. But his eyes dropped again almost immediately, back to his book, and he pushed a tube of cream over the table-top without looking up from the printed page, his voice dismissive.

'Use this. With that fair skin of yours you'll burn up if you don't.'

Furiously annoyed, both with his obvious disinterest in her and her own hurt reaction to that dismissal, she plonked down on a lounger, unscrewing the cap of the tube of sun lotion.

If he'd had any designs on her at all, he would have insisted on helping her to spread the lotion over the parts which were difficult to reach, at least. But he was ignoring her, not even noticing her contortions, and...

Appalled by her thoughts, she slapped the tube down on the table, her soft mouth set in grim lines. She didn't want him to notice her, to make advances, to have designs. Of course she didn't. The very idea was crazy! Sexual overtures from him were the last thing she wanted!

Nevertheless, it would have been very gratifying to be in the position to slap him down...

'Help yourself,' he suggested, still not looking her way, indicating the tray of drinks Sabine must have brought out, his voice stealing quietly into the drowsy afternoon air. Christa stared at him suspiciously. Did she detect a thread of amusement in his tone? Was that a quirk of humour beside his mouth, making him look even sexier, if that were possible?

Probably not, she decided huffily. He was obviously immersed in his book, enjoying it. She hoped so, for his sake. She wasn't prepared to have him laughing at her.

Crashing about a bit, she half filled a tall glass with crushed ice from the freezer jug, covered it with gin, added a dollop of tonic and two thick juicy slices of lemon.

Swallowing it in three thirsty gulps had been a mistake, but not an entirely unpleasant one, she decided five minutes later as she stretched out gracefully on the lounger. She was so, so sleepy. A sleepless night, the travelling, the wedding, all that emotional trauma...

She woke to a totally new and quite delicious sensation. Every bit of her was relaxed, receptive, and she moved languorously, beginning to identify the source of the overpowering sensation—warm fingers were sensuously stroking a slick of sun lotion over the top, exposed part of her breasts. Gliding gently, the sure touch feather-light, sliding now into the valley between the twin globes that were hardening, pushing against the filmy fabric that only partly covered their urgency.

Oh, my! Her heart set up a furious patter as she felt the lounger depress beneath his added weight, felt the warmth of a hard, fabric-covered thigh rest against her own as he shifted his sitting position beside her, one hand now resting intimately against the smooth satin curve of her inner thigh, the other dipping beneath the fabric of her swimsuit, curling to cup one swollen breast and then the other.

'Christa...'

His voice was thick with desire—he knew how his ministration with the oil had aroused her and was taking full advantage! She knew she should fight him off but

somehow her body refused to conform to the dictates
of her mind. The emotions he was arousing were far too
strong, blinding her to sense and logic. She simply wasn't
ready to slap him down yet, she told herself hazily. Her
body was still half drugged with sleep, too languorous,
too yielding... And she was shaking inside with a need
far stronger than anything she had ever believed herself
capable of experiencing...

Tentatively, she opened her eyes, just a little, and between the heavy fringes of her lashes she saw that he
now wore faded denims, riding low on lean hips, clipping
muscular thighs, and an entirely involuntary moan left
her throat thickly. She didn't want him to know she was
fully awake, fully aware of what he was doing to her,
because as soon as he did she would have to make the
painful effort to push him away. It would be quite fatal
if he ever knew how easily he could make her forget her
principles...

As he bent over her, her mouth parted helplessly and
her eyes drifted shut as he touched her lips with his, just
touched, until, as if he couldn't hold back, as if the sheer
incendiary heat that was pulsing wildly through her blood
was claiming him, too, his mouth took hers hungrily,
his tongue stroking hers, his hands discovering every part
of her body, gentling her, as if she were a frightened wild
thing.

But Christa wasn't frightened, far from it. She was
exultant. Nothing remotely like this had ever happened
to her before. She was not herself—she was a creature
of fiery liquid sensation beneath his hands, his mouth.
He was teaching her things about her body she hadn't
known before. And the sensory bombardment was too
much for her to cope with so, with a small purring sigh,
she gave up the attempt, her arms going around his naked

shoulders, holding him to her, her mouth a passion-swollen pout as he lifted his head, murmuring thickly,

'My beautiful, beautiful Christa...' Then his breath caught on a rough gasp as his hands deftly pulled the narrow straps from her shoulders, exposing her full breasts to his hungry eyes. 'My God—I want you! All of you. And I know you want me, I've know it since I kissed you at the reception. Don't ever fight it again—you're mine, Christa. Mine!'

As his glossy dark head bent to her breast, his mouth fastening with near reverence around one swollen peak, Christa froze. She had known he had correctly read her response to that kiss—he was too experienced to have missed something as obvious as that. But to hear him put it into words had brought her to her senses with a vengeance. He knew he could make her respond to him on a physical level, if she allowed him to come near enough. And it was degrading.

Her body might demand that he satisfy the wanton need that he had so expertly and effortlessly aroused in her, but her mind told her that she didn't love him, he didn't love her. The only aftermath would be shame.

And one word would do it. Just one word, the right inflexion, a pretence of wakening from an erotic dream...

Clamping her lower lip between her teeth in an effort to counteract the overwhelmingly exciting sensation his moistly suckling lips engendered, she made a supreme effort of will, moved her head slowly from side to side, and murmured huskily, 'Howard... Darling Howard...'

CHAPTER EIGHT

'I'M ENTERTAINING my French partner, Philippe Recaud, and Fleur Moreau, my interior designer, at Tinkers this evening. I shall want you to be there, so be ready to leave at eight,' Ross informed her coolly.

Christa eyed him warily. Since the episode at the poolside, four days ago, when she had allowed him to believe that the only reason she had responded to his kisses and caresses had been because she had been dreaming she was in Howard's arms, she had seen very little of Ross. Hardly anything, now she came to think of it.

By the time she came down for breakfast Ross had disappeared on one of the business forays that kept him out, or so she was supposed to believe, until after she had gone to bed. And she had always been asleep, or pretending to be, when he got into the bed that was the twin of her own.

His neglect of her wasn't surprising, not in the circumstances—what did surprise her was that she should feel neglected! That was something she was going to have to work on.

From what had happened at the poolside she knew that the sort of surface-friendly, platonic marriage she had in mind wasn't on the cards as far as he was concerned. She had agreed to marry him and he quite fancied her, so she might as well share his bed—that was the way he would see it. And that kind of reasoning didn't merit house-room in her head. This wretched marriage would have to remain thorny, with no room for ordinary friendliness or companionship.

He was formally dressed this morning so she supposed he had delayed his departure for work for long enough to order her to accompany him this evening. But she didn't want to go anywhere with him. If they couldn't be friends, and he couldn't accept that the marriage was to be in name only, then she didn't think it wise, or safe, to spend any more time in his company than she was obliged to.

Seating herself carefully at the opposite side of the wrought iron, white-painted table, she gave him a frosty glare, only moderating it fractionally when Sabine appeared with her breakfast tray of coffee and fresh fruit.

'Still here, Ross? Shall I bring an extra cup?' the Frenchwoman enquired brightly, as if the unexpected sight of the grim-faced man had made her day. But Ross frowned, his hand making a slashing, rejective movement. 'Not for me.'

Not one whit abashed by the curtness of his tone, Sabine gave him a warm smile before turning the lightly veiled hostility of her eyes on Christa, who pretended not to notice, feeling, although she couldn't have said why, pleased that Ross was as snappy with Sabine this morning as he was with her.

'And wear something other than those eternal jeans,' he instructed tersely when Sabine left them alone together, his silver eyes frowning dismissively over her light blue cotton trousers and black sleeveless T-shirt. 'Anyone would think you didn't possess anything else.'

'I don't,' Christa replied with an airiness that said much for her self-control. Who the hell was he to tell her what to wear! 'At least, not here,' she added on.

She was pouring herself a cup of coffee when he extracted a wallet from an inner pocket and slapped what looked like a small fortune in notes down on the tabletop. And her hand shook, but she didn't spill a drop of the dark aromatic brew when he grated, 'Then go out and buy yourself something suitable.'

'I don't see why I should,' she said flatly, beginning to feel like an over-coiled spring, although she'd be damned if she ever allowed him to see that he could affect her in any way at all, and tacked on acidly, 'I don't feel like going out tonight. I never did go a bundle on works outings.'

'My God!' Suddenly he was on his feet, anger staring hotly from his eyes, turning them black. 'You have to be the haughtiest bitch I've ever come across—and I've met a few! But I tell you this——' he slapped one fist into the open palm of the other hand '—I'll humble you yet, lady. And that's a promise.' He turned, not looking at her, his mouth a tight bloodless slash. 'Be ready at eight, or I won't answer for the consequences.'

She hadn't seen him really angry before; cold, remote, out of patience with her, but not searingly angry. Even when she'd murmured Howard's name, knowing it was the one sure way of stopping the lovemaking that had been having such a disastrous effect on her, he hadn't shown anger.

He had merely frozen, staring at her as if he couldn't believe what he was hearing, and the shattering look of pain she'd glimpsed in his eyes before he'd levered himself up off the lounger and walked away had almost had her rushing after him, confessing her horrible stratagem, begging him to take her back in his arms again.

Fortunately, she'd come to her senses in time, consoling herself that only his male pride had been hurt. It could be nothing else but that—and frustration, of course. She knew she'd behaved appallingly, and was slightly ashamed of it, but her actions had stemmed from an inner self-defensive mechanism, and his consequent absences from the villa had left her in no doubt that he was salving his hurt pride and working his frustrations off elsewhere. A man with his looks, his magnetic personality, would never have to look far to find some willing female, so she had no reason on earth to feel guilty. And she was sophisticated enough to turn a blind eye to his rovings. She didn't want him, so why should she be dog-in-the-mangerish about it?

So this morning she would explore the harbour, find somewhere quiet for a leisurely lunch and spend the rest of the day exploring further afield, on foot if need be. She most surely wasn't going to be anywhere in sight at eight o'clock this evening. He had ignored her before their wedding, and apart from that abortive seduction scene he had ignored her since. She wasn't about to let him dictate to her now!

Wondering what to do with the money he'd gracelessly banged down on the table, she decided to leave it in the room they shared, for safe keeping. No way would she use it for the purpose he had intended, and she was gathering it up as Sabine came to collect the tray, her dark eyes narrowed with dislike.

The dislike was mutual, Christa acknowledged, turning away. She had tried to be pleasant to the housekeeper, but her conversational overtures had been ignored, her offers of help around the villa turned down flat. Christa didn't understand the other woman's attitude, but she wasn't going to lose any sleep over it.

Anxious to get away from the villa, from an atmosphere which was hostile whichever way she looked,

Christa deposited the money Ross had given her in a drawer, grabbed her bag and made her way down to the harbour. But, oddly enough, the activities, the sight of the luxurious craft on the sparkling blue waters, didn't hold her interest for more than a few minutes. Her thoughts kept turning to her dark-haired, silver-eyed husband, wishing they could at least be friends. Loneliness engulfed her in a tide of sheer anguish and, angrily, she brushed the tears of self-pity from her eyes. Pushing away the futile and treacherous desire to have things said unsaid, and things done undone, she walked briskly into the town and began to window shop for gifts to take back home.

A display of silk shawls took her mind off her miseries, and she chose one in vibrant tawny reds and golds, knowing Tania would love it. More enthusiastic now, she browsed on, only realising as she paid for her father's gift with the last of her francs that it was way past lunchtime.

Tucking the bulky, gift-wrapped black ceramic horse under her arm, she stepped out of the cool air-conditioned shop into the street, lingering under the awning while she balanced her packages more securely.

And then she saw them, walking on the opposite pavement: Ross and a striking dark-haired woman whose long youthful stride exactly matched his loose-limbed pace. Christa's eyes narrowed as she drew further back beneath the shade of the awning. She didn't want Ross to see her. They had parted on far from friendly terms, and the way he'd called her a haughty bitch still hurt. And for some reason she felt strangely vulnerable, at odds with herself. She didn't think she could put on a friendly smile, make small talk, if he saw her and felt obliged to introduce her to his companion.

Besides, Ross was talking to the other woman with a warmth and animation he'd never shown to her, and Christa didn't like it. And she liked it even less when, deep in conversation, the woman caught her elegantly slender high heel on an uneven paving stone and Ross's arm came out, steadying her.

Anyone would have done the same, but not everyone would have turned the instinctive gesture of chivalry into an embrace, Christa thought, seething with an inner disturbance she couldn't quite identify as she watched the unknown woman cling to Ross, her face lifted appealingly to his, oblivious of the stares of the passers-by who walked around them.

Her mouth tight, Christa turned and strode in the direction of the villa, the pain winding around her heart too intense and immediate to be lightly dismissed. She was *jealous*! Blindly, paganly *jealous*!

A few hours earlier she had been telling herself in a dry academic fashion that she was sophisticated enough to turn a blind eye to her husband's extra-marital activities. But reality was something else again. Seeing Ross hold another woman in his arms had woken the sleeping savage in her, and the situation was painful, to say the least.

Back at the villa she off-loaded her packages and wondered whether to make herself a sandwich. But she wasn't hungry—the ache inside her was loneliness. It was a new emotion for her. Even as a child she had been self-sufficient, happy to have company but just as contented without it. Today, though, since her row with Ross, loneliness had grown until, now, the aching weight of it was too much to bear. So she would phone her father; she was desperate for a loving word from someone, and as she dialled from the study where the open double glass doors gave her a view of clipped lawns and the neatly raked gravel of the drive, she wondered where her valued self-containment had gone, and why it had gone.

Her pangs of jealousy at seeing Ross with that woman were smartly dismissed as she listened to the telephone ringing out at the Hall. She hadn't been jealous. No way. Just hopping mad. Angry because her husband was out on the town with some lissom lovely while his new bride kicked her heels, alone and neglected. Far too public a statement of the state of play between them for her liking. Humiliation hadn't been part of their deal as she'd read it.

'Yeah?' A strange male voice spoke into her ear, shattering her thoughts, and she frowned, gripping the receiver more tightly.

'Is that Liddiat Hall?'

'Yeah.'

So she had got the number right. Pushing a smile into her voice, she asked, 'May I speak to my—to Ambrose Liddiat, please?'

'Ain't here, luv. Try later.' The line went dead and Christa's eyes darkened with puzzlement. What the hell was going on? Who was the owner of that roughish male voice? And where was Ambrose?'

Quickly, she dialled Tania's number and the redhead was characteristically gushy when she recognised her caller, not letting Christa get a word in.

'Are you having a fabulous time? Where are you? Not that that matters—being on honeymoon with a man like that husband of yours would turn hell into heaven! He's absolutely super! And you made a fantastic couple—yours was the only wedding I've ever cried at! But I'll tell you something—you're sadly missed, not only by yours truly, but Howard's going round with a face like thunder and a temper to match. I think he must have a secret yen for you, he's been like the proverbial sore-headed bear ever since the wedding...'

Finally Tania ran out of steam and Christa stated her reason for calling.

Tania said drily, 'Oh, that—not to worry. Ambrose must be off looking at breeding stock. He's quite his old self again, you'll be pleased to know. Apparently, your too, too divine husband is setting him up in business again—breeding and training hunters. Given him *carte blanche* by all accounts—with the proviso that Ross's own financial managers keep a grip on the business end of matters—and the guy who answered the phone would have been one of the team of builders. They moved in the day after your wedding. But surely Ross told you all about it?'

Ross hadn't told her a thing, not a thing, and Christa listened to some more gossip about the amount of money that was being poured into the restoration of her home, then made her excuses and rang off.

So he was keeping his side of the bargain—had set her father up in business again, doing what he knew and loved best. The extent of Ross's generosity, his caring, overwhelmed her, somehow deepening her sense of loneliness. That was pouring money into the work on the Hall meant very little to her.

She met her reflected eyes in the gilt-framed mirror above the telephone table. Large, haunted, violet eyes. Honest eyes. And she read the message they contained quite easily. It wasn't his money she wanted, it never had been. She was deeply grateful for what he was doing for her father, but as for the rest—she wanted nothing material from him. She wanted his liking, his respect, his love. *His love?*

Shattered by the blinding self-knowledge, the far too obvious connotations, she turned away from the mirror, from the revealing insight and, with a drily muttered 'Fat chance!' she walked to the open glass doors, dragging in a few shaky breaths of the warm flower-scented air, trying to pull herself together.

Somehow, against all logic, she had fallen in love with her husband. The ruthless, blackmailing go-getter she had painted in her mind had, contrary to all her pre-conceived notions, revealed a highly responsible and caring side of his character that, added to his tre-mendous drive, superb looks and magnetic personality, produced an irresistible whole.

He cared about people—his chef back in London, her father—herself, quite probably. But as far as she was concerned the caring stopped with the material. As long as he was married to her he would ensure that she wanted for nothing, that her former home was fit for a million-aire's wife, that this villa was at her disposal whenever she felt the inclination to use it, that she was superbly fed and, if he had his way, beautifully dressed.

But that was as far as the caring would ever go, for her. He would never love her—why should he? He had virtually bought her and as long as she functioned properly, acting as his hostess and giving him the intro-ductions he so mistakenly coveted, he would be satisfied.

He was obviously a highly sexed man and if she, as his wife, wouldn't allow him in her bed, he wouldn't have far to look for consolation. Women would fall for him in droves.

As if to emphasise her point, two of the women who obviously thought he was the be-all and end-all appeared on the lawns, walking slowly over the smooth turf to the drive. Sabine, who always had a devoted, motherly smile for her adored employer, and the dark-haired beauty who had been sheltered within his arms, the message in her eyes as old as time as she'd gazed up at him, the pair making a vibrant focal point in the busy street.

The two women were walking slowly, deep in earnest conversation. Christa couldn't hear what was being said but she felt hot with temper. What was that woman doing here? Was she in the habit of visiting Ross's French home? Her eyes narrowing, she saw that as they reached the gravelled drive Sabine placed what seemed to be a consoling hand on the other's shoulder, then reached up to kiss her cheek, and stood watching as the younger woman walked away, her stride stiff but rapid as she moved towards the wrought-iron gates.

Impelled by a need to know, Christa stepped out on to the terrace, her mouth tight, her head high as she approached Sabine. And the flicker of dark hostility in the housekeeper's eyes as she turned to face Christa was all she needed to deepen her determination to know. She clipped levelly, 'Who was your visitor?'

She was incensed when Sabine replied frostily, her mouth curling derisively, 'What is it to you?'

Christa took a deep breath. She didn't know what she had ever done to earn Sabine's dislike, but she said unemotionally, 'This happens to be my villa. I have a right to know who comes and goes.' Had it been anyone else, Christa wouldn't have mentioned the subject. She wouldn't object if Sabine had twenty visitors a day. But that particular woman...

As if her claim to ownership, albeit through her husband, had some effect, Sabine's rigidly held shoulders slackened slightly as she muttered, 'Fleur Moreau, my niece. She visits here. Ross knows this,' she added tersely, her eyes defiant as if challenging Christa to make what she liked of the situation.

Christa thought: I bet he knows! And wondered if the swimsuit Sabine had produced a few days ago was one of Fleur's, and if she had worn it for him and they had swum in the pool together, lain on the loungers together, made love...

Her mind reeling with a jealousy she couldn't now pass off as anything else, she said thickly, 'Why do you dislike me so much? What have I ever done to you?' She felt disorientated, lost in a crazy vortex of emotions—jealousy of the beautiful woman who claimed her husband's time and attention, the woman who had free access to his home and to his arms—as she had witnessed that morning. Her own newly recognised love for him was poignant and painful, and Sabine's cold dislike...

'Do you really want to know?' Surprisingly, a small shaft of malicious humour glinted in the black eyes.

Christa said stiffly, 'Naturally, or I should not have asked.'

'I have no dislike for you, personally,' The bony shoulders lifted in a Gallic shrug. 'Just who you are— Ross's wife. He is like a son to me, you understand. I have known him many, many years and he once did my husband a favour... But that is no concern of yours. But I hoped——' the dark eyes turned, lingering on the drive where the other woman had stood '—I have no children of my own and so I am more fond of my sister's child than most aunts. It grieves me to see you take her place. That is all.' Sabine began to move away but Christa stepped in front of her.

'*Her* place?'

'Can't you guess?' the other woman muttered irritably. 'Before he met you, we hoped, Fleur and I, that she would become his wife. She travelled with him almost constantly, she writes to me that she is madly in love with him, that he, well—that he is kind. But then,' again the expressive shrug, 'he is always kind, always thoughtful for others. But I myself have observed them together here, observed and hoped that the two young people most dear to me will marry. But he brings you here as his wife. And you are not what I wanted for him. My Fleur was for him. And you—you make him miserable.'

Christa swung away, her heart pounding. She, too, had observed Ross and Fleur together, and the memory sickened her. She swung quickly over the grass but Sabine followed, reaching out a thin brown hand to grab her arm.

'Wait! Don't turn your back on me as if what I say to you is of no account! I tell you this—you make Ross unhappy, you make Fleur unhappy. It cannot last. You sleep in separate beds, you drive him crazy so that he hides himself in his work all day, and half the night. You are sending him back into Fleur's arms—she will show him the warmth his bride lacks! She is a clever woman and more beautiful than you—also, she is chic—you dress yourself like a student, a mere child!'

'That's enough, Sabine.' Christa spoke with quiet authority, but a pulse beat crazily at the base of her throat. Turning, she walked away. She knew now why Sabine resented her so much, why Fleur had gazed so deeply into Ross's eyes, why he had turned a protective gesture into an embrace.

Recalling his conversation at breakfast this morning, she knew that Fleur Moreau was his interior designer and would be present at the dinner at Tinkers tonight. And she also knew that, despite what she had said, she would be there.

She had no doubt that Ross had already decided to keep Fleur as his mistress and that the French girl wouldn't put up any objections.

But that wasn't going to happen, not if she, Christa, could prevent it!

CHAPTER NINE

As SOON as she was out of the shower and towelled dry, Christa reached for the new set of undies she'd bought that afternoon. Pure silk, exquisitely embroidered, they'd cost a bomb. In fact she'd spent every franc Ross had given her with no trouble at all.

Her dress was hanging on the back of the bathroom door and she stepped into it, pulling up the tiny zip, feeling the soft fabric caress her skin. She had never owned anything as lovely or expensive before. But she'd been determined to find something to knock his eyes out, to make a 'hands off' statement in front of Fleur Moreau, and this was it!

White silk crêpe, it skimmed her willowy body, the subtle hinting at feminine curves far more sensual than a more blatant garment could ever be. With the warm honey tan she'd acquired over the past few days the effect was sensational. All set to contrive an equally stunning hairstyle, she walked into the bedroom, the fabric of her dress swaying and clinging, moulding her body then swaying away again, and Ross, removing his shirt, froze.

Christa froze too. She hadn't expected him to be home yet. And he said nothing, but his eyes spoke volumes as they flicked over her, missing nothing from the deep cleavage that hinted at the curves which clever design work ensured stayed concealed, to the glimpse of the gilt kid of the new strappy sandals beneath the narrow hemline. And she felt very unsure of herself, very vulnerable. Falling in love with him had done that to her.

And, suddenly, she wasn't quite sure how to handle their fraught relationship.

Above the pattering of her heart Christa heard her voice emerge squeakily, 'I didn't hear you come in.'

'You were in the shower,' he answered shortly, his discarded shirt already over the back of a chair, his hands at the waistband of his trousers.

Christa looked away quickly, her face running with colour, and stepped out for the dressing table, almost falling over herself as she forgot the height of her spiky heels and the narrowness of the cut of her ankle-length dress.

Seated in front of the mirror she caught sight of her hectic colour, the glitter deep in the depths of her huge drowned eyes and cursed herself for her susceptibility where he was concerned. If only she hadn't discovered how much she loved him, then this evening wouldn't have mattered. He could have consoled himself with Fleur and welcome. But she did love him, and she could see no way of altering that, she thought defeatedly, hearing the bathroom door close behind him.

Willing her pulse-rate to settle back to normal, she stroked a brush through her riotous silver-gilt hair. If she could complete her make-up in time she could be out of here before he emerged from the shower, and give herself a slice of time, away from his weakening presence, to get herself under control. But the more she scrabbled with pins the more her hair fell down again around her face. Exasperated, she hurled down the brush and caught her hair up in a hank.

Ross said, 'Leave it loose. I like it that way.'

Damn and double damn! He was out of the shower in record time and an entirely unstoppable glance at the mirror revealed that lithe, power-packed body, superbly tanned, still wet from the shower, nakedness only given a token reprieve by a very small towel tucked around his hips.

Smartly lowering her head, she grabbed her eyeshadow, that annoying, betraying colour flooding her face. He had no right to look so sexy, no right at all, and suddenly, because the intimate tension was becoming too much to bear, she began to babble.

'What time are we meeting your friends?' A flick of deep grey shadow, another of violet. Blend. Fingers not quite steady, not steady at all . . .

'As I told you, we're meeting at Tinkers at eight.' Dry voice, cold. He was obviously still punishing her for the way she'd called out Howard's name when she'd been responding so whole-heartedly to his lovemaking. The thought of how she'd turned him off still made her feel queasy, even though she knew she'd done it out of self-defence. She hadn't realised, then, that she was already falling in love with him.

She glanced at the mirror again and was rewarded by his naked back view as he reached into the wardrobe where his shirts were kept. Her mouth dry, her heart thundering like a steam hammer, she took in the wide bronzed shoulders tapering down to the narrowness of waist and hips, the neat buttocks and long muscular legs covered with a fine dusting of dark hair.

Swallowing nervously, she closed her eyes, only to find his image imprinted on her retina. Hurriedly, she reached for her mascara wand, gabbling, 'Why do you call all your restaurants Tinkers?' She knew why—Howard had told her. But the way she'd called him 'scum' and stated that she wouldn't touch him with a ten-foot pole troubled her deeply now. She wasn't a snob, and didn't want him to think that of her. And if he thought she hadn't read that article, the one that had revealed his humble origins, then he might understand that the derogatory remarks had been a natural reaction to his attempts to blackmail her into marriage.

But he dashed all her hopes that he might begin to see her in a better light by asking grittily, 'Don't tell me you're interested in anything about me?'

'Of course I am!' And that was the truth. He was the most interesting personality she'd ever encountered. Strong, caring, devious, straightforward, intelligent, arrogant—the list was endless and mostly contradictory.

He must have picked up the sincerity in her tone because he replied more easily, 'I was brought up in a Liverpool slum, the youngest of a large, hopeless family. My parents never did get around to marrying and we lived in one room in a decaying house. The point being, my lot were so feckless that they were even looked down on by all the other no-hopers. We were known, derisively, as "Tinker" or "Irish", so when I was in the position to open my first restaurant I called it "Tinkers"—cocking a snook at my childhood, I suppose. The name stuck.'

The rustle of clothing told Christa that he was dressing and she felt safe enough to swing round on the stool, telling him, 'I see,' his dry look telling her that he doubted if she did.

He was looking magnificent in a dark silk and mohair suit, a frown drawing his silky black brows together as he attempted to fold his black tie. Christa itched to go and help him; she had done it so often for her father that it was second nature to her. But Ross, with that silly chip on his shoulder about not belonging socially, might construe any offer of help from her in entirely the wrong way. Instead, she asked lightly, 'What happened to your family?'

His tone was wintry as he queried, 'Thinking of asking them to the Hall? I warn you, if either Danny or Rory show up, you'll have to bolt down anything movable or valuable.'

There was such a wealth of bitterness in his tone that Christa flinched, but she coaxed a smile to her voice as she reminded him, 'There's nothing of value left, as you know. You're not the only one with a feckless family! And we'll invite yours, if you'd like us to.' She twisted the wide gold wedding band between her fingers, wondering at her instinctive use of the word 'we'. It implied a togetherness that was completely lacking in their marriage and she regretted that desperately, her eyes darkening with pain as she saw his shoulders relax as he finally managed to fix his bow tie.

One thing was clear about this man—everything he did he had to do to perfection, and on his own. He would never lean, never ask favours, and everything he set his hand to would be perfectly accomplished, which was why this farce of a marriage—which he seemed content to leave in its present shambles—was so out of character for him. It gave her a little hope...

'I don't think so,' he responded to her suggestion edgily, walking across the room, his hand beneath her elbow as he helped her to her feet. Silvery eyes subjected her to an assessing stare then, as if satisfied with what he saw, he nodded. 'We've time for a drink before we leave. Like one?'

'Thank you.' She answered steadily enough despite the tremor of sensation the warm touch of his fingers on the suddenly sensitised skin of her arm produced, tacking on, 'I'd like that.'

Conversation hadn't figured much in their relationship and she knew that only by talking to each other could they grow closer. She wanted that so much. But did he? Probably not.

Nevertheless, when they were seated on two facing sofas in the salon, he with a small measure of scotch, she with the white wine she had asked for, she probed again, 'Have you lost touch with your family?'

'Don't you mean "Have you cut them out of your life because that sort of scum wouldn't fit in with your monied lifestyle"?' he parried coldly, making her face run with colour because she had never entertained such a thought and was angry because he could have thought it of her.

But he obviously mistook her flush for one of guilt and there was an overlay of disgust in his voice as he told her, 'By the time I was fourteen my mother had been dead for two years, my father was well on the way to becoming an alcoholic and we hadn't seen Danny or Rory for years. Danny had done a spell in a remand home and as far as we knew Rory met him on his release and, to all intents and purposes, they disappeared off the face of the earth. And my sister Cathy took off to find our grandparents back in Ireland, and that was the last we saw of her. She was only fifteen.'

She wanted to hold him in her arms, to give him the love she now knew he had never had, and she husked, 'Oh, Ross——'

He didn't seem to hear her and his tone was without emotion as he went on, 'So at fourteen I decided to cut free as well. I went to London, got odd jobs, slept rough, did the sort of work no one else wanted. I was big for my age and wasn't questioned when I said I was sixteen. Eventually, I got a job as a skivvy in the kitchens of a well-known restaurant. It was the sort of place where only the very rich can afford to eat. Up until then I hadn't known such wealth existed and I decided I'd own my own restaurant one day—but it would be even better, more classy. And, as you know, I did—via night classes in business management, learning all I could by watching the various chefs I'd worked under, investing every penny I could spare from my wages on the stock market—plus quite a few I couldn't. Now...' He drained his glass, set it down on a marble table-top and stood up, the perfect male animal, clad in expensive tailoring, in control. 'It's time we were on our way.'

'Ross, I'm so sorry——' Christa rose fluidly, her willowy body in the sophisticated trappings of wealth swaying towards him, compassion for the tough, street-wise, determined child he had been darkening her eyes.

'Don't be.' He turned his back on her, his face a blank wall as he walked from the salon, leaving her to trot in his wake. 'Just before I opened my first restaurant I went back to Liverpool to try to trace my folks. The house where we'd lived had been pulled down and I heard that my father had died a few weeks before in a charity-run home. There was still no trace of my brothers, but I found Cathy. She was in Ireland, married, and on the point of going to Australia to follow her husband who'd been working out there for several months. He's done well for himself and they've got a couple of kids. Cathy says she'll never come back, but I've visited a couple of times and we keep in touch. So you see, my dear,' his tone was blank, 'you have no need to fear an influx of my totally unsuitable relatives descending on your country seat.'

*   *   *

Tinkers, Cannes, was just as exclusive as its London counterpart and the food was divine, the service excellent, the wines out of this world. But Christa paid scant attention to what she was eating, her mind still involved with what Ross had said.

His scathing remark about not having to worry in case his relatives came to sully Liddiat Hall had hurt her more deeply than she would ever have thought possible. Everything seemed to conspire against her to reinforce his opinion that she was a snob of the first water. It was an impression she had to change because, as well as loving him, she admired him whole-heartedly, and she just had to make him understand that he didn't need to angle for acceptance by the county set. Those owners of old money and old pedigrees couldn't hold a candle to him for his generosity, his caring, his intelligence—not to mention his sheer grit and determination.

Seen close to, Fleur Moreau was one of the loveliest women Christa had ever met, and just as clever as Sabine had said. She was also in love with Ross—it was there in every look, in every nuance of body language. Ross would have to be a fool not to know it, and he was far from that.

But Ross was her husband, she loved him, and she wanted the chance to make their unlikely alliance work, so she had no intention of standing by while Ross succumbed to Fleur's charms.

At first the talk was mostly shop. And it soon became obvious that the Frenchwoman, in her role of interior designer retained by Ross, was no slouch.

'So you will give me a free hand in this project, Ross darling?' Fleur enquired huskily in her lightly accented voice.

Ross smiled, the lines bracketing his sensual mouth deepening sexily as he gazed into the melting velvet brown eyes of the woman whose slim white hand was laid possessively over his.

'But of course, as in everything, Fleur.' His voice lingered over her name as if savouring it, as he had no doubt savoured her delectable body in the past—and might be planning to do so again.

Christa was seething with an uncomfortable mix of jealousy and rage, and while the wine they were to have with dessert was being poured Philippe Recaud smiled at her, his black eyes almost disappearing into his round cheeks.

'I think that just about clears everything up.' The portly, middle-aged hotelier's remark had been made with the intention of turning the conversation to more general topics, for her sake, she knew. He couldn't know that his simple phrase could be interpreted on two levels—that Ross's words, the way he looked at Fleur, made the very special relationship between the two as clear as crystal. Or did he know? Was he feeling sorry for her; puzzled, perhaps, by his English partner's behaviour—newly married to one woman yet determinedly holding on to an older love?

The gleam of sympathy she'd glimpsed in Recaud's eyes took on an entirely different meaning. It sickened her. She didn't want anyone's pity. She had never given up on a project in her life, and she wasn't about to begin now.

Fleur might want him for herself, as Sabine had said, and Ross quite obviously cared for the French girl. That they had been lovers in the past almost went without saying. But, she, Christa, was his wife, and that alone gave her an advantage. It also gave her a sense of triumph, as if being his wife in name meant more than she knew it really did. But tonight was only the beginning of her campaign to force him to see her in a different light, to admit the possibility that he could see her as something more than the key to open doors for him.

But Fleur had an armoury of her own, Christa realised, as limpid brown eyes were turned in her direction.

'Forgive me, I must have bored you witless with this talk of my work. You may take your revenge and tell me all about your career. You did find something to do, before your marriage?'

The implication being that anything Christa had to say on the subject would bore the intelligent Fleur out of her socks or, rather, her sheer silk Dior stockings! Christa opened her mouth on the honey-coated acid-drop comment that was clamouring to drip off her tongue, but Ross forestalled her.

'My wife helped a girlfriend in a little dress shop for a time—the sort of frolic suitable for ladies of a certain class.' He was leaning back in his chair, the long fingers of one finely made hand toying with the stem of his wine glass, his silver eyes drifting over his fuming wife with unconcealed amusement, as if he found her 'frolics in a little dress shop' ludicrous when mentioned in the same breath as Fleur's talents.

She recalled how he'd once accused her of never having had to earn her own living, of just 'idling at home with Daddy'. And he was wrong about the boutique, too. There had been no playing around, she'd had to work hard for the wages Tania had cheerfully admitted were a pittance.

If he'd made that remark yesterday she would have been justifiably furious. But now, because she knew she loved the beast, she was more hurt than angry. But that didn't show as, lifting her chin and forcing a wide smile in Fleur's direction, she said confidentially, girl-to-girl, 'Even the most intelligent of men can be such chauvinists, can't they? Particularly with their wives. It suits him to forget to mention that before I was forced to go home for personal reasons I held down a senior secretarial post with one of London's most prestigious advertising agencies.' She paused for a moment to let Ross assimilate that fact, dipping delicately into her wild berry sorbet. Ross hadn't known of the interrupted career, and she was certain Ambrose wouldn't have mentioned it. It had been something he had felt guilty about.

Swallowing the ice was difficult, but not as difficult as finding another easy smile for Fleur.

'As a matter of fact, I was to have been elevated to executive status. Still could be, as it happens.' She turned the insincerity of her smile on Ross and saw he was wearing the closed-in expression that, as she knew, effectively masked a racing mind. She said with pointed sweetness, 'I think I shall probably take them up on the offer—they promised to hold the position open for me. As you know, darling——' a very slight stress of the endearment, '—I've never been one for idling around at home. I have a brain, and I like to use it.'

The atmosphere around the table became very tense, as if the information she had given Ross had tempered his former light bantering with steel, transmitting its coldness to the others.

So he didn't like to be wrong, to realise he'd made mistaken assumptions, Christa thought, putting her own interpretation on his frightening stillness, the coldness of those silver eyes.

Her violet eyes dreamy, her smile carefully enigmatic, she met his brooding gaze and tilted her head so that the candlelight painted highlights of gold in the tumbling fall of her hair, and his wide lower lip quirked as his head dipped briefly in what she might have taken to be a salute of admiration if she hadn't known better.

'It is something we shall of course have to discuss at some future date.'

'Of course.' Christa met the molten silver of his eyes and her smile was entirely natural. Round one to her, she rather thought. The rout of Fleur had just begun.

And it was then, precisely then, that Christa began to flirt with her husband, her lovely eyes teasing, her soft lips parting in silent invitation, her hand often straying to touch his in unspoken intimacy.

And he, to her secret amazement, played his part as if she had primed him beforehand, giving a responsive and wholly flattering reaction to her antics. His response would tell Fleur, she thought, more than any words, that all his thoughts were now for his new wife. She felt elated, on a crazy high, and if the stolid Philippe Recaud was left to entertain one obviously displeased female interior designer for longer than good manners decreed, than what of it?

Such blatant neglect would have been seen as impossibly rude in any other circumstances, but she and Ross were newly married and it was high time both he and Fleur realised that!

The atmosphere in the car during the short drive back to the villa was almost overpowering. She felt on a dangerous high, and whether that was due to the wine she'd had or to her flirtation with Ross she wasn't quite sure. In the company of others she'd been able to get her act together, to behave as the starry-eyed bride. That the act had excited her, as evidenced by the tell-tale fluttering of her pulses and the melting molten feeling that invaded her limbs, was not in doubt.

What was in doubt was his possible reaction. He wasn't a fool and would know why she'd decided to publicly stake her claim on him. What he didn't know was that she loved him, wanted to try to build on the tottery edifice that was their marriage. And when he did speak it was to pull up the subject Christa least wanted to hear about.

'We're very fortunate to have the services of such a talented designer,' he said with such obvious sincerity that Christa was forced to ask,

'Does Fleur work on all your hotels and restaurants?'

She was felinely gratified when he told her, 'Up until now. Though while you were in the powder-room, just before we left, she dropped a strong hint that she might take up a job offer in the States. I'm going to have to try to change her mind.'

Don't try too hard! Christa thought, wondering if her act tonight and Ross's obvious response had been responsible for Fleur's sudden decision. Or was it just a red herring, a ploy to get Ross to 'persuade' her in the way the Frenchwoman wanted most?

As she slipped out of the car she allowed Ross to put an arm around her as they walked into the villa. Inside a single lamp had been left burning and the high, cool hall was dim and silent. Slipping her feet gratefully out of her new shoes, Christa revelled in the coldness of the marble underfoot and padded towards the stairs, very aware of the sway of her body beneath the skimming white dress. Aware, too, of the jolt of electrifying sensation as Ross came behind her, his arms pinioning her to the hard bulk of his body, his hands planted palms downwards on the soft curve of her stomach, his lean fingers splayed, his touch searing through the thin fabric, shattering her composure.

For a moment she was too stunned to move, or too transfixed with earth-shattering sensory bombardment, and then, her breath coming quickly, emphasising the twin peaks of her body's arousal, she muttered. 'It's late. Let me go. I'm dead on my feet.'

But he told her in no uncertain terms, 'You don't get away so easily, my love. You've been promising me heaven and beyond for most of the evening, and it's a promise you're not going to wriggle out of, believe me.'

CHAPTER TEN

HER breath clogging her throat, making speech impossible, Christa found herself gathered up in his arms and
the fact that her own automatically rose to twine around
his neck she put down to the wine she had consumed.
Though she hadn't had that much, she reminded herself
as Ross reached the head of the stairs, his chest not even
heaving—as if he carried such burdens up endless flights
every day of his life. And unfortunately for her peace
of mind she had to admit that the sense of intoxication
she was experiencing was due to being in his arms, and
not from alcohol.

If they hadn't been before, then his intentions as he
carried her into the big master suite and deposited her
on the huge four-poster became quite clear. She wanted
his lovemaking as she had never wanted anything before.
But not like this.

She loved him so much it hurt, but to him she was
just another desirable female body. If she had avoided
the dinner party tonight—as had been her original intention—then, by now, he would have been in Fleur's
bed. She had no illusions about that.

Her heart fluttering madly, she tried to escape but was
pinned to the sumptuous, lace-covered counterpane by
a very determined hand.

'It will be rape,' she warned him throatily, her eyes
huge and dark, her breath coming rapidly.

'No, it won't.' He sounded very sure of himself, his voice dark velvet, heavy and rich. 'You want me as much as I want you. I'm just going to prove it, that's all.'

That's all! Christa's mind screeched as she viewed the implication of his words with growing panic. He was speaking the truth, she did want him. The heavy pulsing of her blood, the wanton arousal of her breasts, the slickness of her loins, the way her mouth was trembling with the need to meet, explore and devour his, were all blatant pointers to a condition which, although she had never experienced it before with any other man, didn't call for clinical explanations! And unless she was very careful, or very clever, he would prove it!

If he had come to her with love she would have welcomed him with unreserved passion. But he didn't love her; he had made it quite clear that he didn't even like her.

His burning eyes holding her rigid with sexual tension, he began to undress, dropping his jacket carelessly on the floor, his hands moving to his tie. Christa groaned inwardly as the spiral of warmth tightened deep inside her. She could not, would not, let him make love to her. He would be using her, nothing more and the experience would be degrading.

With quiet determination she began to wriggle off the bed, to make for the door. He was removing his trousers and, with any luck at all, would fall over them if he tried to catch her. But he was far too quick for her, hauling her back to the bed, pinning her down with his body, one of his hands capturing both of hers, holding them above her head as his body shifted slightly making her vividly, breathlessly aware of his arousal.

'Oh!' she gasped breathily, the wanton sensations coursing through her body making her incapable of uttering anything more telling, and he smiled lazily.

'Oh, indeed.' His eyes softened to something that looked amazingly like tenderness as they roamed her flushed features, her pouting rosebud mouth, the startled violet eyes that glimmered at him between tumbled, bright strands of hair.

With his free hand he pushed the hair back from her face and began kissing her. Teasing kisses, utterly, hopelessly delicious kisses, tasting her lips, feathering across her eyelids, her temples, down the length of her arching throat and back to her mouth to complete the havoc, parting her lips, his own moving oh, so seductively, sending her mindless.

Her body—responsive to begin with—took on a decided will of its own beneath the erotic onslaught of his clever hands and devastating mouth, becoming a wanton thing, demanding, enticing. When he removed her clothing she found her own hands helping him, and then, skin to scorching skin, whatever reservations she might have had were tossed recklessly aside as she gloried in the entirely unsuspected, entirely ecstatic sensations his beautiful male body gently, yet with a passion that blew her mind, introduced her to.

The big bed was blissfully comfortable and Christa stretched lazily, opening her eyes to soft early sunlight. The memory of last night's repeated lessons in rapture made her bones weak, curved her full pink mouth into a dreamy smile.

She turned her head slowly, her bright hair spilling over the pillow, one hand outstretched as languorous fingers idly traced the indentation on the pillow next to hers. Ross. He must have woken early. He was probably showering. He surely wouldn't leave her to immerse himself in his work today! He would come back to her soon, sliding his lean length between the silk sheets, reaching for her... Her warm mouth curved and she closed her eyes, waiting for him...

When she woke again the sun was high and she wriggled out of bed, yawning, stretching her arms above her head, her naked body bearing the rosy flush of fulfilment.

Funny, she thought, regarding her body in the full-length mirror on the wall, she could look at herself and not feel even the smallest twinge of shame for what had happened. She had been so sure that her principles would have her cringing with it, with the disgust that she had believed would come after making love with a man who didn't love her.

But shame, or anything approaching it, didn't get a look in, not yet, as she showered and put on the swimsuit she had borrowed from Sabine, trying to forget that it might have belonged to Fleur. All that was in the past now. Surely Ross couldn't have made love to her last night, the way he had done—so often, passion alternating with blissful tenderness, if he didn't feel something for her? And, after last night, whatever he felt for her could be built on, nurtured.

Ross hadn't rejoined her in bed so he must have found her asleep and decided to let her catch up on the rest which last night's lovemaking had deprived her of. He was a caring man—it was one of the things that had made her fall in love with him, though she had never expected he would show such consideration for her. The thought warmed her and kept a soft smile on her lips as she went down to find him, only to be told by Sabine, who was on her way back from market, that he had, as usual, eaten an early breakfast before leaving to attend to business matters.

That wiped the smile from her face and the expected shame crept in around nine that evening when, deciding he wouldn't be back until it suited him, as usual, she picked at the cold food Sabine had left her and drank more wine than was good for her.

She had been a gullible fool to imagine that last night's forbidden rapture could have made any difference to the way he felt about her. He was a caring man but the caring didn't extend to her. He had bought her, or as good as. She was a useful commodity and nothing was going to change that.

Last night wouldn't happen again, she vowed as she made her way upstairs at eleven. She couldn't stand the way it made her feel. He had used her body because she, in his arrogant opinion, was his property, was available, had been willing. But not any more. Not until he at least learned to like and respect her. But hell might well freeze over before that happened!

Feeling ill with misery, she dragged off her clothes and burrowed into the single bed that had been hers since she'd arrived here—apart from last night. And last night was something she was going to have to forget.

But in spite of her determination, the memories came flooding back when she woke to find herself being scooped into strong, resolute arms, and carried to the big room, her naked flesh responding wickedly to his.

She tried to command him to put her down, to take his hands off her, but the only sound to emerge was a throaty groan. At that, his arms tightened around her as he kissed her with an almost hostile impatience that scared her witless. He didn't need to use the gentle art of seduction to make her mindless with wanting him. And that was what frightened her most.

Showing no compunction whatever, he slid her into the big bed, his voice a rough statement, 'This is where you belong. Here, with me. Not in that lonely little bed, dreaming of Howard.'

It was the only time he'd mentioned that name and it should have made her wary, but the magic had hit her by then, enveloping her, rapture flooding her as his mouth moved over hers, his hunger drugging her, her arms moving instinctively to hold him, because she loved him, her body melting into his as his hands rediscovered every inch of her with exquisite possession.

The pattern of lonely days and passion-filled nights continued. If Ross returned for dinner, which he did on two occasions only, he treated her like a stranger. He was polite, but no more than that, and their tempestuous night-time need for each other was never even obliquely mentioned, never acknowledged by word or touch. It was as if the magic, the rapture, was a secret shameful thing, only leaping to vigorous life behind locked doors. His attitude made Christa shy, oddly gauche, in his presence.

After they'd been at the villa for ten days she pulled herself together enough to make a stand. He was using her and her love for him was such that she secretly welcomed the magic-filled nights she spent with him. But her life couldn't go on like this. Their relationship wasn't progressing the way she longed for and she had to try to push it on to a more emotionally rewarding plane.

Willing herself to wake before he did, she found her eyes sliding open at dawn and she heaved herself up against the pillows, memories of the previous night's lovemaking turning her voice husky as she said his name and stroked his naked shoulder with her fingers.

'Ummm?' he murmured sleepily, turning on his back with lazy animal grace, and Christa's mouth went dry. He was so beautiful. His strong jawline was dark with beard growth just beneath the tanned skin; his mouth relaxed, utterly sensual, his dark hair endearingly rumpled, his strange silver eyes languid as if drugged by the sleep that was the narcotic aftermath of a deep and tearing need now satisfied.

Her eyes drifted helplessly over the breadth of his shoulders, the satiny bronze skin roughened by crisp body hair across his chest, angling down over the flat planes of his stomach to be lost beneath the thin silk sheet that had become tangled around his lean hips and long legs.

Her throat tightened, her heart hammering out a drum-beat tattoo. Except for one abortive occasion their intimacy had been confined to darkness, and now...

'What time is it?' The transformation was remarkable, she thought sadly, as his eyes snapped to cold, clinical alertness before he growled the question at her and swung his legs over the edge of the bed.

'I don't know. Early.' She scrambled out of bed, too, pulling on her robe. Having made up her mind to it, she wasn't going to let him escape so easily.

Following him to the bathroom as he turned on the shower, she almost turned tail and ran, because if one look could have turned her to stone, they'd have had to chip her off the floor! But she wasn't a quitter and they couldn't go on like this, because she couldn't stand switching from shame to sexual abandonment with clockwork regularity. She reached up and turned off the shower, enduring his hostile glare, and told him, 'I want to talk. It's far too early for even you to start the working day. And talking of which...' She had walked back to the bedroom, half holding her breath in case he decided to ignore her, lock her out of the bathroom and get on with his shower. But she heard him follow her and finished off, 'Do you have to work today?'

'Why do you ask?' The painfully polite daytime mask was back in place and he had pulled on his own robe which made things easier than if he had stayed naked.

'Because we spend so little time together,' she answered quickly. 'We never have time to talk. I don't see you all day. This is supposed to be our honeymoon,' disliking the utterly sickening, plaintive note that had crept into her voice, biting her tongue to stop herself from doing any more demeaning whining.

He flopped down on the bed, his long legs stretched out, his arms crossed behind his head. He closed his eyes and said drily, 'And there was I, thinking you had everything you could possibly need.' When she gave a small derisive snort, because she surely didn't know what he meant by that, he said flatly, 'Not even you could accuse me of neglecting you at night, and Sabine tells me you pass your days in the idle luxury I'm sure you enjoy— by the pool or in it, eating, drinking, soaking up the sun. Don't tell me there's something missing?'

At least he had been interested enough to ask how she spent her time, and that was something, she supposed. She took a deep breath and said honestly, 'Your company.'

Just for a moment he seemed to go very still, to hold his breath, but he soon shattered the illusion of a man recently stunned by shifting his body as if to find a more comfortable position and drawling sardonically, 'Bored, are we? What do you suggest?'

The old Christa would have suggested watching him jump off the edge of a cliff, for starters; the new, desperately loving one said, 'We could spend the day together.'

The statement was simple enough, surely, so why did he seem to take forever to consider it? And when, his eyes still closed, he asserted blandly, 'So we could. How does a day at sea grab you?' Christa had to stuff her fist against her mouth to prevent a childish whoop of joy from escaping.

'Lovely,' she managed at last.

She didn't mind at all when he instructed dismissively, 'Get dressed. I'll catnap until you've made coffee.'

Bossy! she thought, smiling. She hadn't felt this happy in ages. And after she'd showered and pulled on the borrowed swimsuit, covering it with a white halter-neck top and a wrap-around black cotton skirt, she padded down to the silent kitchen to make coffee, put out the fruit she preferred for breakfast and searched for eggs to scramble for Ross. She found she was singing. For the first time ever she felt like a wife.

The day could have been perfect if Ross hadn't persisted in treating her like a barely tolerated guest.

'I have permanent use of the *Water Baby*,' he told her as he led her aboard the gleaming yacht lazily riding at anchor in the harbour. 'She belongs to a friend of mine and I use her when I'm here.'

'She's beautiful,' Christa enthused. 'Have you taken her out often?' She wasn't going to admit that a day spent on this graceful craft, alone with Ross, was her idea of heaven. Their uneasy relationship had to make progress before she could begin to think of telling him how she felt about him.

He told her off-handedly, 'She's fully crewed,' but the fact that they weren't, after all, to be alone together wasn't the cause of the knife-thrust of agony in her chest. That followed his comment, 'The last time I availed myself of Griff's million-dollar toy was back in the spring. Fleur and I spent three days cruising.'

And three nights making love, Christa agonised. No wonder the other woman looked at him with devotion, had decided to put herself on the other side of the Atlantic when she learned he had married. Ross wasn't a man one could make love with and then forget—as she knew to her cost!

The pain inside her chest would have had her doubling up in agony had she not been made of sterner stuff. Imagining Fleur sharing Ross's bed made her feel ill. But she wasn't going to let him know how jealous she was. She couldn't cope with his amusement.

'How nice.' Her lips formed the words stiffly, despite her intention of making the remark sound casual to the point of indifference, and her reward was a briefly intent look of surprise before he took her arm, showing her over the luxurious craft and introducing her to the crew.

Most of the day was spent exploring the coastline and she tried to ignore his cool politeness, the shuttered look in those silver eyes whenever they were turned in her direction. He was distancing himself, she realised, and far from bringing them closer, as she had hoped, the time they were spending together was, moment by moment, driving them even further apart.

She had desperately wanted to establish a better relationship, she thought miserably, declining to join him in the sea when the yacht anchored off Monte Carlo in mid-afternoon. Everything was going wrong, she mourned as she stroked sun oil over the tanning skin of her long, elegant legs. She didn't have to work out the reason for her dejection. Mistakenly she had hoped they might be able to form some kind of rapport, something to help him to grow to like her instead of merely lusting after her body, something that might, in time, grow to more than liking...

Eventually, Ross hauled himself back on board, water running in sparkling rivulets from his magnificent body, and she caught her breath, loving him so, and was only able to offer him a slight, wobbly smile as she invited him to share the freshly made iced lemonade the steward had brought her.

'No, thanks.' He gave her a frigid look and added with cruel sarcasm, 'Our day out has worked wonders. You're about as lively and sparkling as a hibernating bear!'

'I'm sorry——' She didn't know why she was apologising when her misery was all down to him, and her huge eyes swam with humiliating tears.

He muttered tautly. 'This has been a mistake. I'll go below and suggest we put back into Cannes.'

'No!' The cry was involuntary. Sometimes, as now, he looked as if he thoroughly disliked her, as if he was as ashamed of their unbalanced relationship as she, and she didn't want the day to end like this, in total failure. She had so much hoped for something to grow from their time together, but today had proved how impossible that hope had been. He didn't want to get to know her as a person in her own right. He wanted nothing from her except social acceptance and her body in his bed. And Fleur to turn to when the pleasures of the marital bed palled? an unwelcome voice nudged inside her brain. Lust soon faded when love was absent.

He turned abruptly then, his eyes narrowing as they took in her obvious distress.

'Oh, God!' he muttered between his teeth, then hauled her to her feet, holding her at arm's length, his features taut as she tried to blink away the shameful tears. Their marriage was without love, on his side, which was why she was feeling over-emotional, out of kilter. A sob rose in her throat, and she gulped it back, tears brimming over from dark-lashed violet eyes, her mouth trembling, and Ross swore softly, pulling her against his naked chest, his hands moving soothingly over her heated skin as he murmured gently, 'Don't cry, kitten. I won't pack you off home if you don't want to go. Shall we put into Villefranche and stretch our legs?'

He was treating her like a child, she realised, her tear-wet cheeks pressed against the solid wall of his chest. He was coaxing away what he would see as brattish tears with the promise of a treat. But she didn't mind. She felt cossetted and cared for, and that was something totally new in this strange marriage. Impulsively, her arms crept around him, her fingers splayed against the warm satin of his skin. If he thought that she could break into tears because of something as trivial as a cut-short outing then so be it. For the moment she simply wasn't up to arguing.

'That was delicious!' Christa wiped her fingers on her napkin, her eyes sparkling. The devilled king prawns had been superb, a speciality of the tiny restaurant overlooking the harbour, the house wine rough and gutsy. But her mood had nothing to do with the food or the wine. It was all down to his change of attitude.

Wandering through the steep ancient streets hand in hand, sampling the coffee at one of the many cafés, peering into the shops, with Ross insisting on buying her a tiny black bikini—so she could return the borrowed swimsuit, he'd explained with a light in his eyes that had belied his sober reasoning—had made her feel, at last, that they were a couple.

And that was important to her, a beginning, no matter how small. 'Coffee, Christa?' he asked, smiling at her across the small table, candlelight mellowing the harsh cast of his features.

She nodded, wanting to reach out and run her fingers over the masculine planes of his face, but contented herself with just touching his hand as it lay on the cloth near his wine-glass.

'I'd love some,' she told him, her voice husky as he half turned to catch the waiter's eye, his lean fingers twining through hers, not letting the contact go.

'Then home to bed.' He turned to her again, his lazy smile knocking her for six, leaving her in no doubt that sleep was the last thing on his mind. 'You're looking very beautiful, kitten,' he told her softly, his eyes skimming over her very ordinary cotton top as if the fabric barrier were non-existent. 'I can't wait.' Gently, he lifted her hand to his lips and placed a small kiss in her palm, making her heart kick with unstoppable excitement. It was the first time he had made any reference to the erotic, silent lovemaking that filled their nights and his words bonded them together, made their relationship closer.

Smiling absently as the waiter brought their coffee, Christa decided to go one step further. For the past few hours Ross had been indulging her; true, this tender, almost loving mood had emerged out of the tears that must have seemed so out of character and childish to him. But if she could persuade him to treat her like an adult now, to talk about their relationship, then there might be a chance of making their marriage a real one, something of value.

She was tired of the tension of loving him, knowing he didn't return the emotion, tired of the niggling shame she felt because she enjoyed being made love to by a man who, she knew, was only using her. Resting her elbows on the table, cupping her chin in her hands, her eyes serious, she watched as he stirred his coffee and asked, 'Ross, what do you want out of this marriage?' And then, because that didn't seem the right jumping-off point, because she knew what he wanted and that was social acceptance through her, plus a female body in his bed if that body happened to be willing, she tried again. 'When we married, did you have any idea of how long you wanted it to last?'

She could have bitten her tongue out when she saw the bleak cold mask cover his features, heard the frigid quality of his voice as he wanted to know, 'Why do you ask?'

She didn't know how to put it into words and could have wept all over again at the change in him. She hadn't meant it to sound as if she wanted out of their marriage, of course she hadn't—she loved the brute, didn't she? She had merely wanted to know how he felt about things, how he thought. It was the only way they could go forward.

How could she tell him that she was afraid that the time would come when she had outlived her usefulness, when he would know himself accepted by the people he wrongly thought mattered? That when that time came he would want to be free to marry a woman he could love, have children to inherit his very considerable wealth. How could she say these things and betray her own feelings? It was too soon. He wouldn't want the burden of her love.

'I suppose you want me to eventually give you a divorce so that you can go back to Howard?' he questioned brutally. 'No way. "Darling Howard" is going to have to do without you.'

The cruelly dismissive line of his mouth was enough to tell her that as far as he was concerned the subject was closed. Closed before it had ever got started. So much for her stupid hopes!

'For how long?' Her voice was very cool. Whatever he chose to think, the subject wasn't closed—not until their future had been sorted out. And if he wanted to go back to being her enemy then that was fine by her. Because right at this moment she wanted to hit him, she wanted to cry, but she could do neither, of course.

Her temper rose to boiling point however, as he snapped, 'For as long as it suits me. Let's go, shall we?' He laid his cup on his saucer and reached in the back pocket of his jeans for his wallet.

Christa sat exactly where she was, refusing to budge while he persisted in treating her like a mindless possession that had suddenly become tiresome. Her stubborn chin lifted as she said cuttingly, 'I haven't finished my coffee, but if you want to wait outside then please feel free to do so. I might be quite some considerable time.' She saw him subside back in his seat, the look he shot her one of total exasperation.

For a terrible moment she bitterly mourned their earlier closeness, but she couldn't show him that weakness. There could be no looking back, only forward, and they had to talk this thing through. Stirring her unwanted coffee, she remarked bluntly, 'You insisted on marrying me, regardless of how I felt about it, so now you're going to have to put up with me. Tell me,' she added, forcibly bright, 'weren't you taking a terrible risk? I mean,' she expounded, in danger of wearing a hole in the bottom of her cup, 'when you came across Dad, up to his eyes in debt and too frightened to know what he was doing, you must have thought it was your birthday and Christmas all rolled into one. You wanted something and saw a way of getting it, and——'

'What do you mean?' he interrupted icily. 'What did I want?'

Startled by the ice which was devastating, even for him, she glanced up, shrugging, and saw the tense muscles of his shoulders relax as she said, 'To get the right introductions to the right kind of people, of course. What else? You knew Dad, or so you said, and you must have known he had a daughter. You set marriage to me as the price for paying his debts. But for all you know, I could have been a hag.'

'The risk was there,' he admitted tersely. 'But not the way you see it. I'd seen you once, at Ascot, so I knew you were—presentable. We were introduced. You looked straight through me.' He slapped some notes down on the table to cover the bill. 'In my book, beauty comes from within—and in that I was taking a considerable risk,' he tossed with a bitterness that made her catch her breath.

She gaped at him. She remembered Ascot last summer. Gold Cup day. The women in their finery, the men in morning suits, top hats. She'd only gone because she'd known her father was going, and she'd wanted to keep an eye on him. In free-spending company he tended to go over the top at race meetings. She hadn't wanted to go, she recalled. It had meant taking a day off work.

Plus she'd developed a splitting migraine. She hadn't
been taking much in, so Ross could be right when he'd
said she'd looked straight through him . . .

'You were a haughty bitch then, and you haven't im-
proved.' Ross left the table, looking down on her,
warning, 'As soon as I board the *Water Baby* we'll be
leaving for Cannes. You can come with me or walk. It's
entirely up to you.'

CHAPTER ELEVEN

'I HAVE to talk to you.' The words burst out on a rush of pent-up breath. Christa had been determined to wait up for Ross, no matter how long it took, and it was past midnight when he finally walked into the villa, the jacket of his dark grey suit hooked over his shoulder, his tie undone.

'At this time of night?' He stood in the arched doorway of the salon, a single standard lamp throwing a nimbus of light around Christa as she uncoiled herself stiffly from one of the sofas.

'If you must stay out all hours, what can you expect?' she flung shrewishly, hiding her hurt. She wasn't going to mention her suspicions, that he had spent the evening with Fleur, trying to 'persuade' her out of accepting that other job offer. He would not see faithfulness as an intrinsic part of their marriage and to accuse him would only draw attention to her jealousy, a jealousy he would only view with contempt since, as far as he was concerned, love, on either side, didn't enter into their relationship.

Last night, after the things he'd said to her in the harbour-side restaurant, she had fully expected him to leave her alone. But he had taken one look at her as she had emerged from the shower and had dragged her into his arms with a smothered groan. His lovemaking had been wilder than ever before, taking on a new dimension, their frenzied need opening doors to a new and even more demanding sensuality. It had been an experience that had left her shaken, completely submerged in him.

She had still felt shaken when he had rolled out of bed at an impossibly early hour this morning and it had been much later when she had woken properly, able to face the day, to face what she knew of herself, of Ross, of their relationship. But the long hours alone had given her time to think and now she said crisply, 'When we get back to England I intend to take up my job again.'

'Really?' His smile was laconic as he sauntered further into the room, dropping his jacket over a chair.

'Yes, really!' Christa snapped hotly, her determination to take up her career again given new impetus by what had happened yesterday. It was obvious that he would never like her, much less love her. She couldn't spend the next few years of her life—until he had no further use for her—eating her heart out for what could never be. Work, her career, would be a way of subduing the pain.

'I could use your London flat,' she told him, her recklessness increasing by the second beneath his cold, unblinking silver eyes.

His mouth hardening, he swung away to pour himself a brandy. Turning back to her, cradling the glass in one hand, he told her flatly, 'You're my wife. You don't need to work. And where I go, you go. And as I intend spending as much time as possible at Liddiat Hall it follows that you will be there with me. There's no question of your staying in the London flat without me.'

'Why?' Colour surged over her skin. 'I want a life of my own. I won't sit at home twiddling my thumbs until you decide to call it a day. I won't be used——'

'I paid a hell of a lot for the privilege of *using* you,' he stressed cruelly. 'And I aim to get my money's worth.

Besides, who said anything about calling it a day? Not me. The comforting fallacy of a divorce exists only in your warped imagination. I married you, and, as far as I'm concerned, it's for keeps.' He threw his brandy to the back of his throat and slammed the glass down. 'You can forget your dreams of sliding out of our arrangement and taking up where you left off with Howard Mortmain.' He stalked out of the room, his back rigid.

Christa sank down on the sofa, her mind knocked out of gear. That he should view this marriage as a permanent thing came as a complete shock. She had always believed that it would last only as long as she was useful to him. Since she had realised she loved him it had been one of her greatest dreads because no man in his right mind would want to tie himself for life to a woman he didn't love.

But then he probably didn't know what love was. He certainly hadn't known it in his childhood, and since then he would have been too busy proving himself to have time over for the softer emotions. The thought made her feel inexpressibly sad. She wanted to teach him to love, to make him happy. He was capable of caring—that was one of the facets of his many-sided character that had drawn her to him. But capable of loving?

'It's late. Are you coming to bed or do I have to drag you there?' The deep incisive voice cut through the painful miasma of her thoughts, making her leap out of her skin. He had reappeared in the archway, his features stony, and because she knew he would carry out his threat she rose reluctantly to her feet, uncomfortably aware of the shameful welling of excitement that tingled through every vein at the thought of the silent night-time ecstasy that neither of them could deny.

Tight-voiced, his mouth turned down derisively, he told her, 'I'm leaving tomorrow for Rome. After that—Venice, Florence, Madrid, back to Rouen. While I'm in Europe I may as well visit all my commercial properties. It could take four, five weeks in all. You can either come with me or stay here.'

He seemed imbued with a quality of watchfulness, of waiting. It frightened her almost as much as it puzzled her. He was an enigma—she would never understand him in a million years. She looked directly into his hard face, trying to fathom what he wanted from her, what was going on behind those beautiful shuttered eyes. But his features told her nothing, and that was nothing new. He'd been confusing her, manipulating her, ever since the first time they'd met. He was disturbing, powerful, shattering her senses with hidden challenge.

She mumbled, 'I'd rather go with you.' She saw the tension seep out of him then wondered why she'd said that, because four or five weeks free of his demanding presence, his demanding sexuality, would have given her time to come to terms with the way she felt about him and with this one-sided marriage of theirs in which all the odds were stacked against her.

Paris again. Later today they would be flying home after six weeks of hopping round Europe. Six good weeks, Christa admitted, briskly drying her hair, knowing that breakfast had already been brought to their suite.

Visiting Ross's restaurants and the hotels he partly or wholly owned had been an eye-opening experience, increasing, if that were possible, her already great admiration for what he had achieved. And she had happily donned her secretarial hat when Ross had idly suggested she might like to sit in on his meetings, take notes.

They had worked well together and if he had seemed surprised and then delighted by her competence, then she had been delighted too, almost flustered, by his unstinting praise when he had listened to her first suggestions, building her confidence in this new area of expertise when he had taken them seriously, turning them over in his active brain, accepting most of them, urging her to voice her opinions, treating her as though her contributions had real value.

Belting the silk, kimono-style robe which Ross had bought her in Rome, Christa shook her head, sending her still damp curls flying around her shoulders, and left the bathroom. Ross looked up from the table by the window in the sitting-room, his smile slow and appreciative, warming her, making her body tingle beneath the whispering caress of the gold-coloured silk, and he said, 'You look warm and golden—like an apricot,' and put the paper he'd been reading aside, pouring coffee from the silver pot.

For a moment Christa stood quite still, halfway across the room, her small tanned feet rooted to the carpet. She looked at him across the room, at the night-dark silkiness of his hair, the beautiful decisively chiselled lines of his features and her heart turned over with love for him.

And that was nothing new, not for her. And neither was the pain of knowing he would never love her.

'Looking forward to going home?' he asked idly and she nodded, smiling. She *was* looking forward to going home. Stupidly perhaps, and against all the odds, she felt that under their own roof things might conceivably be different. They might grow closer. And she hoped that working with him, as he had promised she could do, would help to forge bonds. She wasn't ready to give up all hope yet.

'Tremendously. I can't wait to get back,' she told him and watched his face harden, as if her admission had angered him.

He said curtly, 'I wonder why? Anything to do with Mortmain?'

She shivered, the brightness suddenly going out of the day. And the feeling persisted until they were back at the Hall and she was confronted by all that had been achieved in the two months they had been away.

Ambrose was on the main steps to greet them when Ross had parked the Lotus Elan on the newly gravelled sweep in front of the house, but he made it clear that he was only the welcoming committee. The living-quarters above the stable block, which Ross had had renovated for him, were so compact and comfortable that he never wanted to go back to the main house.

'And Mrs Perkins!' Christa gasped as Ross, his hand cupping her elbow, guided her through the newly decorated hall. 'And the portraits!' She lifted bewildered eyes. 'But Ross—how?'

'Welcome home!' Mrs Perkins called chirpily, hurrying towards them, clearly enjoying Christa's open-mouthed bewilderment. 'I've got the kettle on the boil; shall I take tea through to the small sitting-room?'

'That would be fine, but make it in half an hour, would you, Mrs Perkins?' Ross replied, and to Christa, who was torn between gaping at the housekeeper she'd known all her life and had never thought to see again and at the family portraits which had had to be sold but which were now, miraculously, back in their rightful positions, he remarked, 'Let's take a look over, shall we? Then tea—though from the look of you, you could use something stronger!'

'But Ross, how?' she repeated half an hour later as they walked down the newly restored flight of wide oak stairs. What she had seen had taken her breath away. Liddiat Hall was as she remembered it as a very young child—only more so. Pieces of furniture that had been in the family for countless generations had been replaced and others, which she didn't know but which perfectly suited the size and age of the house, fitted comfortably into newly restored rooms which had been denuded of anything saleable years ago.

From what Tania had said she knew he had been pouring money into the restoration of the fabric of the house, but this—this magical transformation was something she hadn't been prepared for.

'I don't know how you did it, but it must have cost a fortune,' she breathed, clutching on to his arm because her legs weren't too steady.

'A minor one,' he admitted, closing his hand over hers as it held on to her arm and she loved him too much to do anything but smile at his smug yet impossibly endearing grin as he told her, 'I wanted it to be a surprise. I had three weeks to organise everything before the wedding—with your father's help, of course—and as soon as we left on our honeymoon—which I deliberately strung out—the architect I'd briefed moved in. He did all the hard graft, organising the building teams, the decorators——'

'But the furniture, the paintings—so much of it is family stuff. Some was sold years ago!' Christa still felt as if she were in a dream, that she might wake at any time and find herself back in the Liddiat Hall she knew best—with slates missing from the roof, rain-water dripping through cracked ceilings, empty dusty rooms where memories of past splendour were the only lonely inhabitants.

And was it possible, *remotely* possible, that this arrogant yet caring man, this much loved man, had done all of this to please her? It was a thought she didn't dare dwell on too much, and he said, 'I know,' and grinned down at her flushed face. 'Luckily, quite a lot of the stuff was "important", as they say in the antique trade, and therefore easily traceable. I had two or three scouts out with instructions to buy back what could be found, if possible, and to choose pieces which would fit in sympathetically if a particular item couldn't be traced or if the owner wasn't prepared to sell. Fortunately,' he led her across the hall, 'that didn't happen too often. The dealers I had acting for me weren't given any limits.'

Christa was too overwhelmed to speak. The fortune he had admitted to spending couldn't have been minor at all! And she wouldn't have thought the transformation possible; even if his finances were limitless, time hadn't been. She supposed bemusedly that money bought time, and she knew then, if she hadn't known it before, that for Ross anything was possible.

'Lost for words?' Ross enquired drily as she sank into one of the linen-covered, overstuffed, blissfully comfortable chairs in the small sitting-room that hadn't contained anything other than dust and cobwebs the last time she'd seen it.

'Completely,' she admitted wryly. He deserved far more than a few words of thanks. Wondering how to tell him how much she appreciated what he'd done, she asked impulsively, her heart pattering insanely because he might—he *just* might—say he'd done it to please her, 'Why did you go to all this trouble and expense——?'

He cut her off smoothly, 'Why do you think?' He seemed to be waiting for her answer, as if what she might say would be important, and the tension was suddenly there again.

She didn't know how to answer him. She'd never been able to judge his motives—he'd always been an enigma—and she was grateful for the interruption when Mrs Perkins brought the tea and a rich, home-made fruit cake to have with it. She would have liked to be able to say that he'd restored her home because he cared. That it was his wedding gift to her. But that would be jumping the gun because no matter how romantic it would be, how flattering to a woman in love, it simply couldn't be true. She knew it couldn't because now she was over the initial shock she was able to think logically.

He had started wheels turning before they were married. He had hardly known her, except by sight. To have planned so carefully, spent so freely—all to please a woman—he would have had to have been head over heels in love with that woman. And that simply wasn't so.

'Well?' he prompted as soon as Mrs Perkins left them, and Christa, pouring tea, felt the tension like a sharp and tangible thing. She hated the cat-and-mouse game that had been the hallmark of their relationship, the hidden motives, the secret undertones, and, more than ever, she longed for total openness between them, longed to be able to tell him exactly how she felt about him, to try to make him understand that she wasn't the haughty bitch he believed her to be. But now wasn't the moment—the silver eyes held the familiar shuttered, watchful expression, blocking her out. She sighed. For the time being she would continue to play the game by his rules.

'Because you wanted the Hall as near as possible to how it was in its heyday, because money spent on property, on good antiques, is a better investment than most?' She gave him the answer she thought he expected to hear. A sensible answer, with no messy emotional undercurrents. She passed him his cup. 'Plus, you are going to want to entertain—we'll have to return all the hospitality that's going to come our way, and we couldn't have done it in any style if the house had been left in the state it was at the time of our marriage. Try some of Perky's fruit cake—if she hasn't lost her touch it will be delicious.'

She passed him a plate, looking at him now because she hadn't wanted to before, not while she'd been second-guessing his reasons, not when he might have seen the regret in her eyes. She would have liked it to be so very different. And she wasn't prepared for the bleak coldness that looked out of those arctic eyes, not prepared at all. The loss of the warmth, the approval of the last few weeks hurt her as nothing had ever hurt her before. And his cold words, 'You are quite right, of course,' sounded a death-knell for whatever small hopes she might have had.

For what was left of the day he remained aloof. He was courteous though, very, and it made her want to scream. She didn't know what was wrong. It was as if something she had said had triggered a reaction, taking him even further away from her.

She dressed carefully for dinner that night because it was a homecoming, a celebration. Her father was joining them for the meal and he, because he loved her, might know how hurt and confused she was feeling, and she didn't want that.

Descending the stairs, knowing she looked cool and sophisticated in the flame-coloured draped chiffon sheath Ross had picked out for her in Paris, her silky curls tamed into an upswept Edwardian style, she met Ross on his way up, taking the stairs two at a time.

For a sickening moment her heart seemed to stop, then raced on, making her feel she'd just run a marathon. He was still wearing the hip-hugging faded jeans he'd changed into after they'd unpacked and he looked through her, as though she wasn't there, only pausing long enough to apologise distantly, 'I lost track of time. Sorry.'

And that was that. That was all. And she carried on down the stairs, trying to look as though she weren't in mourning for the precious measure of closeness they'd achieved while travelling though Europe. But she did care of course. She cared until it hurt because she loved him. Loved him.

Her father made up for any restraint at dinner. He couldn't stop talking about the horses he'd acquired for breeding and training, and Christa, pushing Perky's excellent roast lamb around her plate, wished he'd change the subject.

The money to acquire the animals had obviously come from Ross, and much more would have to follow if the expansion plans her father was eagerly discussing with his cool eyed son-in-law were to be realised. It made her feel uncomfortable, guilty. Ross had spent so much, so thoughtfully—quite apart from clearing her father's debts, which must have been horrendous. And what had he received in return? Not much, she had to admit. The opportunity to mingle with county society, and that was about it.

But all that would have to change, she decided suddenly, declining the trifle. When she and Ross were alone she would tell him how she had grown to love him. She had to do it. The pretence had gone on long enough. She knew he didn't love her but if they were to continue to live together then they needed honesty between them, at least. And she would set the precedent by telling him of her love for him.

It would take courage, she knew that. Whatever his faults, he wasn't a monster and he might believe that the burden of her love was too great to carry, offer her a divorce as a kindness, not wanting to tie her to him when he knew he could never return her love. She didn't know how she would cope if he decided to play it that way. But, whatever the result, she had to tell him and later, when they were in bed, the intimacy, the searing passion neither of them could control, would make the telling easier.

Perky had just taken the coffee through to the small sitting-room and as they rose from the table Ambrose said, 'I've just remembered—a mass of invitations came while you were away. The whole county wants your company, Ross. I put them in the study—won't be a tick.'

Watching her father hurry away with more bounce in his step than she could remember, Christa put her hand on Ross's arm, feeling his muscles tense beneath the fine linen of his lightweight jacket.

'Thank you for what you've done for Father,' she said simply. 'Up until a few years ago, and particularly after Mother died, horses were his whole life.'

'Save your breath.' He moved away, as if he didn't want her touching him, didn't want her gratitude. 'Perhaps his talent in the breeding field will keep him away from gambling in future.' His voice was bleak, his eyes bleaker, and Christa could have wept. The hours that must pass before she could tell him she loved him, and could try to build on that, seemed too many to be endured.

But Ambrose was returning with the invitations. She pinned a smile on her face and swept towards him, taking the bundle of envelopes, and crying 'How lovely!' acting as though she couldn't wait to open them when the reverse was true. But Ross wanted them, the type of invitations she held in her hands had been his reason for marrying her, after all, and so, for his sake, she had to pretend to be pleased.

And as they settled down with their coffee she read them out for Ross, her painted smile for him because he was the one who wanted to attend these boring society shindigs—anything from a cocktail party at Grange Manor, to afternoon tea with Colonel Withers-Aspill and his wife to meet the local parliamentary candidate.

Normally she would have run a mile rather than accept any one of the invitations but, for Ross's sake, because it was part of the bargain and because she loved him, she would be at his side, very gracious, very proper.

She sighed and Ross tapped a gilt-edged card with a reflective forefinger, 'This one we can't miss—Lady Maude's birthday party.'

'I don't suppose you want to miss any of them,' Christa returned brightly, doing her best to look cheerful over the dreary prospect. 'I did warn you—we'll get more invitations than we can handle for a while. And then, of course, we shall have to return the hospitality——'

'I'll leave you to deal with them, as you think fit. But don't tie me too tightly. I'm going to have to put more than a few hours in at my London head office,' he replied with a remarkable lack of interest, Christa decided, considering that acceptance by the sort of people who had sent these invitations was the only reason he'd married her.

Confused, she subsided back in her chair, sipping her coffee thoughtfully, happy to leave the conversation to the two men, aching for the time when she and Ross could be alone together, but when that time came it didn't work out as she'd wanted it to.

'If you'll let me have the notes you made I'll put in an hour's work before bed,' Ross told her as he secured the bolts on the main door after Ambrose left.

'Of course,' she said very brightly, covering her pain as her heart fell right down to the soles of her feet. And a few minutes later when she'd handed over the notes she'd made in Europe she couldn't keep the plea out of her voice when she asked, 'You won't be too long, will you?'

He glanced at her briefly, clever silver eyes moving from her troubled gaze to the rosebud pout of her mouth, and his lips curled in self-derision. 'I doubt it. I don't think wild horses could keep me from your bed. Especially when you plead so provocatively.'

But he didn't come. She lay awake for hours, waiting for him. But he didn't come. And when she woke to birdsong and sunshine the only indication that he'd shared the huge bed was the indentation of his head on the pillow beside hers.

She showered and dressed very quickly, very on edge. Something was wrong and she didn't know what it was. Never before, even when they'd been fighting, squaring up to each other like adversaries, had he failed to come to her, driven by a physical need as great as her own.

Incomprehensibly, the transformation of the Hall seemed to have driven them further apart. She couldn't understand it—it had been what he had wanted, obviously.

Not in the mood for breakfast, for enduring Perky's chatter, she wandered outside after fruitlessly searching the house for Ross. The sun was hot for September, the air fragrant, and she should have been at peace, happy, but she was too keyed up to relax.

His car was still garaged so he hadn't gone to head office as she had begun to fear, and, her feet flying, she ran to the stable block, her heart lifting because that was where he would be.

But he wasn't. Her father was unsaddling a big bay gelding, sweat darkening his light green shirt, dewing his brow.

'I haven't seen him,' he answered Christa's breathy question, then, wiping his arm across his forehead, his eyes worried, 'Is there anything wrong?'

And because he was happy, content in the occupation he loved, she couldn't confide in him and say she was worried witless because Ross had withdrawn into some dark, impenetrable shell. So she smiled as if she hadn't a care in the world and lied brightly, 'Of course not. I wanted to ask him how many of those invitations he wants me to accept, but it can wait.' She turned jauntily, smiling, 'See you,' and her brisk steps carried her as far as the lawns fronting the house, out of sight of the stable and her father's watchful eyes.

She began to wander slowly back to the house, telling herself to snap out of it. Everything would be fine. It wasn't the first time he had deliberately held himself aloof—she had weathered it then and could weather it now. And their relationship had to change—for the better, she hoped—after she had told him how much she had grown to love him.

Scuffing her feet through the gravel, she felt some of the tension leave her. Ross didn't love her, she knew that. But he wanted her and that was something. And he wanted their marriage to last, he had told her as much in no uncertain terms, so presumably he would be happier with a wife who loved him rather than one who didn't. And from that beginning, much could grow...

She frowned, the sound of an approaching vehicle breaking her thought patterns, but Howard's Range Rover, rounding the curve in the drive, brought a smile of welcome to her lips. He was one of her oldest friends and she hadn't seen him since her wedding.

Shading her eyes from the glare of the sun, she waited while he walked towards her. As handsome as ever, dressed in light cords and a dark shirt, his blond hair bleached even paler by the sun. She would show him over the house, she decided. She wanted to tell the world what a wonderful, considerate husband she had, but the words died in her throat because Howard's laid-back, easy charm was missing, his features intent, unsmiling.

'Howard—lovely to see you.' Her own smile was wobbling by now and it faded altogether as he stood in front of her.

His eyes were accusing as he snapped, 'Is it? I wish I could believe that.'

His glance raked her body and suddenly, for no good reason that she could think of, she wished she were wearing something more concealing than the ice-blue cotton sundress, the low scooped neckline supported by the thinnest of straps.

'How about some coffee?' she offered, wondering where all the old camaraderie had gone, knowing he wasn't in the mood to be shown over the house, to hear her rhapsodise over all Ross had accomplished.

He followed her inside and only when she reached out to press the bell in the small sitting-room to summon Perky did he break his brooding silence.

'No coffee. I didn't come to socialise.' He paced the room, scowling, and Christa sank into a chair, her eyes bewildered. This surly man wasn't the Howard she knew, had practically grown up with.

'The work Donahue put in hand here, and the money he must have spent, have been the talk of the neighbourhood.' He twisted round, his eyes deriding everything he saw. 'Is that why you married him?'

Christa gasped, horrified by his blunt approach. Was that what everyone thought? If so, it was a rumour that had to be scotched. No one must ever be allowed to even *think* he'd been married for his money. It would demean him, and he didn't deserve that.

'No,' she said coldly, the initial heat of dismay flooding out of her face, leaving her features rigid with denial.

'Then why?' If there was a note of anguish in Howard's voice Christa wasn't interested in hearing it, but she did her best not to flinch away when he sat on the arm of the chair she was using and took her hands in his. 'Three weeks before you were married you asked me to pretend we were lovers,' he said thickly. 'It certainly wasn't for your father's benefit and the only other witness was Ross. So you were trying to warn the guy off and the next thing I knew,' his hands tightened on hers, making her wince, 'I was opening an invitation to your wedding. Has he got some hold over you? Is that what it was?'

His voice had lowered, taking on a husky quality that might have worried her had she not been grappling with the implications of his words. He was too near the truth. The truth that had existed at the time of her wedding. She had married Ross because she had had no option, but she was going to stay with him, fight to make the marriage a good one, because she loved him. And for her father's sake—for all their sakes—no one must know the truth.

Pulling her hands away from his, massaging her crushed fingers, she got to her feet, trying to smile, to look amused.

'What an absurd idea!' She denied the truth of what he'd been saying, hoping she'd convinced him, and he stood up too, taking her arms roughly, his fingers biting into her soft flesh.

'If he doesn't have some hold over you, the only conclusion I *can* draw is that you married him for his money. My God, Christa, you could have come to me! Everyone knew old Ambrose was skint—I could have helped. I'm not exactly on the breadline!' His sherry-coloured eyes glittered feverishly and she pulled away from him quickly because something about his ragged breathing disgusted her. She opened her mouth to deny his accusations, to tell him she loved her husband, not his money, and saw Ross standing in the open doorway.

Her heart kicked wildly against her ribs and one hand went instinctively to cover it.

'Ross——' Her voice was thready, a weak supplication, but he looked like a stranger, the hard lines of his face austere.

Briefly, he dipped his dark head in Howard's direction, 'Mortmain.' Then, speaking to Christa but not looking at her, 'If you're having coffee, ask Mrs Perkins to bring mine to the study.' He turned, leaving them alone.

And Howard said sulkily, 'Surly devil!'

How much of the conversation had Ross overheard? Christa wondered distractedly. Howard had been accusing her of marrying Ross for his money, and while Ross wouldn't like the implication he would know it wasn't the truth. She had married him because he had forced her into a corner, he knew that. But what he didn't know—and *must* know—was that she had grown to love him dearly. Turning to Howard she forced a brittle smile, her voice very cool, very polite, 'You won't stay for coffee, I think you said. So, if you'll excuse me, I have a million things to do,' and spared a brief regret for the horrible change in their long relationship as she watched him stump out of the room.

But the regret was only superficial. The most important thing in her life was Ross.

She made the coffee herself, not bothering Perky who was stirring a pan of damson jam, the rich fruity smell filling the kitchen.

'It's like a dream come true. I never thought I'd see the day when I was back here where I belong. I'd have stayed on, working for nothing—you know that. But I need to earn something against my old age.' The housekeeper kept up a running commentary on the state of her happy situation. 'We're to have two part-time cleaners, did Mr Donahue discuss it with you? Yes, 'course he has! And a full-time gardener. He asked me to put the word about locally and I could name half a dozen who'd jump at the chance. Shall you want to do the interviews?'

'No, you see to it,' Christa smiled. She wouldn't take Perky's moment of glory for the world! 'You know what you're looking for—you are the housekeeper, after all.' She went out with the tray, leaving a very contented lady behind.

She felt shaky as she walked to the study. Her whole future depended on how Ross received what she had to say. She knew she wouldn't be able to bear it if he told her he didn't want her love, and then proceeded, in that frighteningly cool and detached way of his, to cut her out of his life. How many other women had whispered words of love to him? Fleur, for one, of that she was certain. And look how far it had got her!

But she, Christa, was his wife, and he'd stated that the marriage was to be permanent, and that gave her a boost of much needed courage, calmed her racing heartbeats just a little.

He was working, his dark head bent over a pile of papers, and he didn't look up as Christa slid the tray on to the end of the huge desk, his only acknowledgement a muttered thanks. Taking a deep breath to calm herself, Christa looked around. Essentially, the room was unchanged. The panelling had been cleaned and polished, the bookshelves emptied of her father's horse-breeding tomes, and a very high-tech computer had been installed. Otherwise, it was exactly as it had been.

Gradually, her heartbeats returned to normal. Absurd to feel so keyed-up about telling her own husband that she loved him and wanted to make a stable marriage out of a beginning that had once seemed so hopeless, that she was happy and willing to devote her whole life to him and, hopefully, to their children, that she would be patient, hoping he would eventually learn to love her...

'Well?' He looked up, the lines of tension on his face making him look tired. But his eyes were flat, expressionless, not even hinting at an impatience for the way she was hovering.

She smiled nervously, her breath catching in her throat. God, how she loved him, even at his most distant!

Needing to be close to him, to have the reassurance of his warmth, she went to stand behind him, twining her arms around his neck, laying her cheek against his so that the glittering brightness of her hair mingled with the midnight darkness of his, and she breathed huskily, 'Ross. I love you. I've never said that to any man before, and I mean it with all my heart.' And she moved her lips so that she could taste the roughness, the slight saltiness, of his skin, knowing there was so much more to say but unable to find the words because her heart was too full, her throat clogged with emotion.

'Do you?' His lips barely moved, his voice still, tight. It echoed the tension of a body suddenly rigid, totally ungiving, and she sensed the rejection like a physical blow, heard it in the caustic tone of his voice. It made her feel ill.

She straightened slowly, hardly daring to move, not understanding, not yet, blood thundering in her ears as he calmly put down the pen he had been using, telling her acidly, 'Don't you mean you love my spending power? You're no fool, I'll give you that. You know which side your bread's buttered. The only thing you love about me is my bank balance.'

'That's not true!' The words were shocked out of her. She stumbled back a pace or two, her arms held tightly around her body as if to hold herself together.

'No?' He swivelled his chair round, his eyes objective. 'You knew I wasn't exactly short of money when we married. But I didn't hear any pretty words of "love" until now. Why was that, I wonder? Because, since coming home you've learned exactly how wealthy I must be, learned that I'm not averse to spending some of it to please you. So no more protestations of love, Christa.' He sounded weary beyond bearing and he returned his chair to its original position, knuckling the bridge of his nose. 'I don't need or want them. I much prefer it when you're not being hypocritical.'

Tears welled in her eyes, choking her throat. She wanted to crawl into a dark hole and cry the hurt away. But no amount of tears could ease the hurt she felt.

'Money has nothing to do with it,' she said thickly. 'You have to believe me!'

'Do I?' he enquired coldly. 'I wonder why? Do I seem that gullible?' His voice could have fractured stone. 'Only a matter of weeks ago you were asking how long I wanted this marriage to last. It was obvious you couldn't wait to be rid of me, to fulfil your side of the bargain and split. And not half an hour ago I overheard your boyfriend accusing you of marrying me for my money. You didn't rush in to disabuse him, and no doubt he knows you well enough to understand such motives—but he didn't seem too happy about them,' he added drily. 'And while we both know exactly why we married you might as well be honest enough to admit you've suffered a sea-change and are now willing to make it a permanent arrangement because you've had a taste of what real money can do.'

Seen from his viewpoint, her confession of love had to be suspect, she admitted frantically, and unless she could make him believe her now she might as well write their relationship off as a total failure. Moistening her dry lips, she said huskily, 'Doesn't our lovemaking tell you something? I couldn't have given myself to you the way I did if I hadn't been in love with you.'

All her heart had been in her words, willing him to accept the truth, because whatever else happened he had to believe that she wasn't the sort of woman who would lie about a thing like that—and for such a mercenary reason.

But he grated, 'Just what kind of an idiot do you think I am?'

The harshness of his voice filled her veins with ice. He picked up his pen, dismissing her. 'It's not unknown for women of your class to enjoy a little rough trade now and then. Just don't treat me like a fool. It disgusts me.'

CHAPTER TWELVE

LADY MAUDE was holding court, a small yet flamboyant figure, sitting on a chair that resembled a throne at the far end of the huge drawing-room. She was swathed in black velvet, despite the unseasonable closeness of the late September night, and dripping with diamonds in old-fashioned settings.

The whole house seemed trapped in a time-warp, as if the years between the present day and the height of the Edwardian era had never existed, and the effect was enhanced by the bewhiskered members of the string quartet who played with great gusto and feeling behind a screen of potted palms.

Christa smiled edgily as she accepted a glass of champagne from a passing waiter, forcing her wandering attention back to what the group of people around her were saying. All old acquaintances, no surprises. Couples were dancing on the parquet in the hall, and Ross was dancing attendance on Maude.

Apart from one cocktail party and one Sunday brunch, Ross had pleaded pressure of work, asking her to decline all the other invitations. And that had thrown her because the getting of such invitations had been his sole reason for marrying her.

Lady Maude's birthday party was different, of course. Ross had taken a liking to the outrageous old biddy. Even so, right up until the last moment Christa had thought he wouldn't be in time. He had slept at the London flat the night before—too busy to waste time travelling, he'd brusquely informed her, only returning in time to have a shower and change.

He often stayed in London now, she thought drearily, the dark smudges beneath her eyes mute testimony to the strain she was under. Not that it made much difference. When he was at Liddiat Hall she scarcely saw him except at mealtimes. He hadn't made love to her since they had returned from their European trip. Their marriage was effectively over.

Not that she wanted him to make love to her, she reminded herself staunchly, trying to ignore the pain that had been gripping her heart in its cold iron fist ever since he had flatly refused to believe that she loved him. There was now no point in continuing in this sham marriage and when she could get herself together she fully intended to resume her work with her old employers.

Anger at his crudity when he had accused her of making love with him because she had a yen for a bit of rough trade had had her moving back into the bedroom that had been hers in her childhood. And sadness had been her bedfellow because she knew he would never come to her as a lover again. As far as he was concerned, she didn't exist.

'Dance with me, Chris?' Howard was already swaying on his feet, his eyes not quite focused. But he took the untouched glass of champagne from her hand, giving it to his father who was one of the group, and drawing Christa through to the large hall which had been cleared for dancing.

It was a foxtrot, the music seductive, and Christa went into his arms, feeling tearful. She had never been one to resort to tears, but love had changed that. Love changed everything. And she felt the long skirts of her aqua silk dress whisper around her legs and knew an almost irresistible desire to lay her head against Howard's shoulder and confide all her misery.

But all such weakness rushed out of her, jealous anger filling the void, as she saw Ross dancing with a stunning redhead in a flame-coloured dress she seemed to have been poured into. One of Lady Maude's many great-nieces, she recognised, with her arms draped around his neck, her voluptuous body practically fused with his, an attitude Ross was obviously quite happy with!

She should be in his arms, not some blatant redhead! Ross should be holding her, their bodies moving as one, but ever since they'd returned from Europe he had stopped wanting her. His lust for her had burned itself out, he had tired of her, it was as simple and as humili-ating as that.

Never having loved her, and her initial refusal to let him touch her having been overcome, his attention was now turned to new sexual adventures. Not that the redhead would prove to be much of a challenge—more of a pushover, Christa decided acidly, in a frenzy of jealousy as she watched a flame-coloured bottom wriggle closer into the lean masculinity of Ross's hips.

As the sickening, demeaning pain of jealousy knifed its way through her she stumbled, and Howard's arms tightened around her, his breath warm against her ear as he suggested, 'Shall we get out of here, find some fresh air?'

The floor was already uncomfortably crowded and she knew she couldn't bear to watch Ross with the redhead a moment longer—not without resorting to physical violence. So she said 'Why not?' her voice flat, and al-lowed Howard to steer her through the dancing couples and out into the blessedly fresh night air.

Beyond the semi-circular frontage of the house, a flight of stone steps led down through an overcrowded shrubbery to a terrace overlooking immense lawns, silver in the moonlight. Howard paused, leaning against the low stone balustrade.

'This is better. I'm beginning to find Maude's annual thrashes a bit of a bore. But your husband was obviously enjoying himself.'

'He enjoys your great-aunt's company,' she replied tightly, hating being reminded of exactly how much Ross had been enjoying himself.

But Howard persisted, 'He's enjoying Sophie's more. She's a rapacious man-eater, that second cousin of mine, but no doubt Ross can cope. He's had plenty of experience.'

'I don't know what you mean,' she replied crisply, unwilling to let anyone, even Howard, guess at the jealous rage that was making her feel murderous.

'Don't you?' Howard's voice was low and insistent. It was very quiet out here—a faint rustling of the wind in the top branches, a distant echo of the music from the house, that was all.

Christa shivered, the breeze cooling her body through the thin silk of her dress, and Howard pulled her roughly into his arms, his voice thick as he muttered, 'If you'd needed money so badly, you should have come to me. I may not have Donahue's financial clout, but I get by. I'd have taken care of you, you know that.'

'Please—don't!' Christa pleaded breathlessly. His arms were like iron bands, imprisoning her, and the wetness of his mouth as he stopped her protests sent a shock wave of revulsion through her. It gave her the strength to push him away.

'Why not?' He made a clumsy grab for her, ripping one of her slender shoulder straps in the process. 'You know how it's been for me, ever since we kissed the night you asked me to behave as if I fancied you rotten. It stopped being an act the moment I held you in my arms.'

'No!' she denied, horrified, shaking her head wildly. 'It was only an act,' she stressed, gasping as she felt his hot eyes on the moon-silvered upper curve of the breast revealed by the torn strap. 'I was stupid,' she told him shakily. 'Like a child, a selfish child.' She had had only one thought at the time—to show Ross he couldn't have things all his own way. She hadn't thought of the possible consequences. In the past, when she had helped Howard out of a tight spot with a woman who was becoming too marriage-minded, the simple act of touching hands, of looking deep into his eyes, had been enough to warn the woman in question that Howard had his sights set on other game. Christa had always thought the exercise to be slightly cruel, but Howard had assured her that his former lover had refused to stick to the rules and that drastic tactics were needed. Now she deeply regretted the impulse that had led to her asking him to do the same for her!

'Howard—I hate myself for bringing this on.' Oh why hadn't she thought of the possible consequences! 'But really, it was only a game. We've know each other all our lives—we're more like brother and sister.'

'It may have started out as a game.' He took her hands, squeezing until the rings she wore bit into her flesh, then jerked her towards him. 'But that one kiss made it deadly serious for me.'

'Then I'm sorry.' She bunched her hands against his chest, trying to push him away, her whole body rigid with disgust at what was happening, with dislike for

herself and the stupid plan that had triggered this scene.
'I love Ross,' she pointed out breathlessly. 'I'll never
love anyone as I love him.'

'Then you're a fool,' he bit out savagely, gripping her
arms still but holding her slightly away from him,
deriding her with his eyes. 'He doesn't give a rap for
you. And if the way he was blatantly lapping up Sophie's
explicit attentions back there doesn't convince you, then
perhaps you'd better ask him what he was doing with a
certain luscious brunette last night!'

The sneer in his voice shocked her to utter stillness
and the sudden, unwanted pity in his eyes held her rooted
to the spot. She didn't know what he was talking about,
she didn't want to know. The knowledge would bring
her that final step to the end of her marriage, to the
death of all the hopes she'd once nurtured so fiercely.

But Howard forced the facts on her, his voice low.
'He was dining with her at Tinkers last night. I was there.
And if we must resort to euphemisms, they seemed very
close, rather more than just good friends. She was—is—
extremely lovely. The conversation was kept muted, they
were capable of that much discretion—but I did catch
her name—Fleur—and she had a rather seductive French
accent.'

Christa stared at him, the blood rushing through her
head. She couldn't speak. Her voice was trapped somewhere in the lump of pain that was lodged in her chest,
a pain that grew until she thought she would explode
under its pressure.

So he was seeing Fleur again, here, in London. All
those nights he'd spent away had been spent with her!
No wonder he hadn't needed to seek physical release in
her bed! He was an extremely virile man—she didn't need
to have witnessed the way he'd been dancing with Sophie,

only hours after leaving his long-term lover, to know that! Oh, how she hated him!

The dull roaring in her head increased and her legs felt like water. Howard caught her swaying body, holding her close, his voice a dimly heard murmur as he told her, 'Divorce the bastard. I'll always be here for you, Christa, you know that.'

And then the world exploded. Howard was flung back against the stone balustrading, emitting a grunt of pain, or shock, as his body slid to the ground, his legs spread-eagled, and Christa felt her feet leave the paving slabs as Ross hauled her against the hard length of his body.

He didn't say anything, he didn't need to. Stark violence glittered in his eyes, his mouth clamped on a tight line, his nostrils flaring with dark rage.

And before she knew what was happening he was marching her back to the car, her ankles twisting beneath her on her high spiky heels and, apart from a savage expletive as he bundled her into the car, nothing was said until the five miles to Liddiat Hall had been rapidly covered.

He cut the engine while the gravel was still spattering on the gleaming bodywork and bit out tersely, 'You can have your divorce. Mortmain's welcome to you.' He slid out of the car, slamming the door.

Tears of outrage and shock silently covered her face, blinding her as the darkness swallowed him. She sat motionless, the time passing of no importance, and then came the devastating sense of loss, the finality of it all, and it ripped into her, tearing her apart.

Emotion galvanising her—she scrambled out of the car, running towards the house on tottery legs, brushing the tears savagely from her face as she entered the hall.

And Ross came out of the study, his harsh face shut-tered as he dumped two briefcases on the floor.

'I'm taking my personal belongings now. I won't be back,' he told her grimly. 'I never want to see you again. You can have this house and everything in it. And Howard can have you, with my blessing.'

He looked as if he could kill her, his eyes a hating silver glitter in the frozen mask of his face, and she re-pudiated instinctively, her voice dreary, 'I don't want Howard.'

'That's not the impression I got half an hour ago,' he snapped, his eyes stabbing the broken shoulder strap. He made to push past her on his way to the stairs, but something stopped him, made him turn back to her, his eyes contemptuous as they raked her pale, tear-streaked face.

'You were eager enough for him before you realised he couldn't offer the same material benefits I can,' he derided. 'So if I've spoiled your plans to keep me sweetened and cuckolded at the same time, tough!'

He turned sharply, striding away from her, taking the stairs two at a time and she stared after him, hating him, loving him; acknowledging, finally, that their marriage was over.

The slam of his bedroom door brought her out of shock. She may be down, with all the odds against her, but she wasn't out. Not quite. She kicked off her non-sensical shoes, raced up the stairs, and arrived in the master bedroom they had never properly shared, her skin scarlet with exertion and temper, her hair a silver-gilt wildness about her face.

She might still love him, despite everything, but she wasn't going to let him trample all over her!

'How dare you accuse me, you—you two-timing bastard?' she flung at him, wanting to slap him when he glanced up from the suitcase he was hastily packing, a look of distant scorn on his hard features.

He was incapable of real emotion, she decided furiously. While she was boiling with it, her heart pounding out of control, her veins seething with the hate that was the other side of love.

She couldn't tell him of the love, because he refused to believe it existed, but the hate—oh, yes, she was free to tell him all about that!

'You turn my stomach!' she spat. 'You calmly accuse me of wanting Howard, of planning God knows what infidelities for the future, and all the time you're blithely continuing your sordid little affair with Fleur Moreau and setting up another one with Sophie!'

She stamped towards him, her eyes glinting defiantly, her small hands clenched. If she had the strength she would pull him apart, limb from limb!

He straightened up slowly, his face grim. 'Sophie was being an embarrassing pain,' he admitted, his voice edged with temper. 'I had to be downright rude to get out of her clutches when I saw you slope off with Howard. And you've got rocks in your head if you imagine I've ever made love to Fleur.'

'Oh, no?' She couldn't think why she was goading him like this, or why she was listening to his lies. He was leaving her, divorcing her, and nothing was going to change that. But her temper, devilish when roused, wouldn't allow her to leave him to his packing, to walk away with dignity, not while she still had some self-respect left. 'What about the cruise you told me you took together? Three days and *nights* on the *Water Baby*.

What about last night? You were seen together at Tinkers. And Sabine told me——'

'So?' he cut in, the downcurve of his mouth brutal. 'I took Fleur on a short cruise because she was burned out. She needed to relax completely, she'd worked herself into the ground—apart from which, not long before, her brother had been killed in a particularly horrific road accident. As she is a valued employee and *friend*,' he stressed bitingly, 'I could do no less. And yes, I gave her dinner last night.' He tossed an armful of shirts into a case. 'I wanted to talk her out of taking that job in the States. I failed, but it was worth a try. Had I been planning to have her in my bed we would have eaten in my apartment, not in the public restaurant. I should have thought that was obvious, even to you. I've never touched Fleur in that way, never wanted to. It might suit you to believe I'm playing around, to excuse your own extra-marital activities——'

'There aren't any!' Christa stormed, stamping her foot, unable to take in what he had told her. If he hadn't been making love to Fleur, why had he stopped making love to her? Nothing had changed and yet, suddenly, he had stopped wanting her.

'Please...' Ross shot her a weary look before bending down to close his suitcase. 'Before we married you weren't afraid to show me that you and Howard had something going. And it was his name you called out the first time I tried to make love to you,' he reminded her bitterly. 'How do you think that made me feel? I used to hate myself for making love to you, knowing you were pretending I was Howard. But, goddammit, I couldn't help myself!'

He raked his hands through his hair, looking bone-weary now, and bent to pick up the suitcase, tossing his house keys on the carved oak blanket box at the foot of the bed. 'It's over now,' he said bleakly, only the glitter of his eyes betraying any emotion at all. 'I've finally conceded defeat—for the first time in my life.'

He turned to the door, his shoulders rigid, and his voice came hollowly, as if he had already gone from her, 'The weeks we spent in Europe opened my eyes to a side of you I never dared believe existed. I suppose they were among the happiest weeks of my life. I began to think you were at last beginning to forget Howard, growing to care for me, really care. But every time I allowed myself to dream a little you brought me clattering back down to earth.'

'And how did I do that?' she whispered, trying to make sense out of what he was telling her. 'I never meant——'

'Didn't you?' he questioned tiredly. 'Whether or not, it worked. To give one instance—it delighted me to see how happy you were about the renovations here. Everything had been done with you in mind. Only you. But all it meant to you was an investment, a place fit to entertain your damn county friends. It made me feel hopeless, the dreams I'd had so much futile fantasising. And when you came to me the next day, all bright-eyed and bushy-tailed after your snug little encounter with friend Howard, and started chirping on about how much you "loved" me, I knew I couldn't take any more. I should have left then.'

The door closed quietly behind him and Christa stood in the centre of the room, staring at its blank surface. She didn't understand what he'd been trying to say, it didn't tie in with what she knew of their relationship. It was like trying to do a jigsaw puzzle with half the pieces missing.

But whatever happened she couldn't let him walk out of her life without learning the truth. Hearing the heavy outer door close prodded her into action, and she flew down the stairs, skimming over the hall, flinging herself out on to the drive, heedless of the way the gravel tore the fine silk of her stockings, cutting her feet.

'Ross!' He was stowing his gear into the rear of the car and he straightened, turning to face her with a reluctance that made her heart ache.

'I didn't lie to you. Not about Howard, not about loving you,' she insisted breathlessly, pride a redundant commodity in her need to know the truth about this man—the man she loved, always would. Everything he'd said had told her there was no hope for them, but she couldn't let him walk away believing the things he did.

But he was very still, as if he were holding his breath, and his utter silence was more frightening than any amount of scathing words could have been. Almost, her courage deserted her. But she remembered the things they had shared, the good things, and wouldn't let him leave her, more impoverished emotionally than he need be.

'There's nothing between Howard and me,' she began firmly. 'When you invited yourself to dinner that night and found me in his arms, it was all an act. I'd asked him to pretend we were lovers because I didn't want you to think you could walk all over me without retaliation. You'd only recently virtually blackmailed me into agreeing to marry you. And how do you think that made *me* feel?' she echoed his earlier question, her voice rising hysterically.

And she must have imagined the strange softening of his features, the almost humorous tug of his mouth, because his voice was coated with iced sarcasm as he came back, 'That figures—you always were a contrary minx.

But was he acting tonight, out on the terrace? Were you acting when you called his name as I made love to you?'

'Yes... No!' Christa shouted in confusion, hot colour scalding her face. 'It wasn't an act tonight, I wish it had been.' She squirmed with embarrassment and guilt. 'We've known each other forever, I didn't think he'd ever look at me in a romantic light. But I was wrong, and I hate myself for that, and I'm sorry, but being sorry doesn't help,' she confessed miserably. Then, taking her flagging courage in both hands she said firmly, 'But I *was* acting when I said his name. I'd been asleep and you were touching me, and I—I wanted you to go on touching me. And I knew I'd end up letting you make love to me—egging you on as well, I guess—and I couldn't let that happen because, then, I hadn't grown to love you. So I said his name, knowing you'd think I'd been dreaming of him. I knew it would be a turn-off.'

'And you were right,' he commented drily, then, slowly, as if turning her words over in his mind, 'But later, you welcomed me into your bed. And, if I remember correctly, you—um—"egged me on". Why was that, I wonder?'

'Because by then I was in love with you!' Christa yelled, exasperated because he wouldn't see the truth, stamping her foot then doubling up in pain as the gravel cut deeply into her flesh.

'Christa—what is it?' Gentle hands supported her as she hopped on one foot, and as he bent to inspect her injured instep she heard him curse.

She started to cry; she didn't want to but she couldn't help it, and it had nothing to do with her aching foot. Gulping sobs tore at her chest and he scooped her up into his arms and strode back to the house, carrying her to the small sitting-room where Perky had banked up the fire for the night.

'Let me have a proper look at your feet,' he commanded, his voice rough, yet soft like velvet. Kneeling in front of her, he made his inspection, swearing low in his throat. Then he straightened, his face drawn, his eyes holding a million troubled questions which were thrust to one side as he told her, 'Stay there, I'll fetch some water.'

Waiting for him, she stared into the fire, shivering from reaction, her arms held tightly around her slender body. He had seemed so gentle, so caring when he'd realised she'd hurt herself, almost as if he loved her. But he didn't, of course. Never had done, never would do.

When he came back with a bowl of water, cotton wool and ointment, she had already mopped her eyes and sniffed her last sniff, and she told him listlessly, 'I shouldn't have gone out without my shoes,' expecting dry agreement.

All he said was, 'You had more important things on your mind at the time.'

She knew that, but was amazed that he should have recognised it, too. And as he knelt down in front of her she had an almost irrepressible urge to run her fingers through the thick soft darkness of his hair for one last time. But she checked the impulse. He had long since lost the desire to make love to her. He wouldn't want her touching him. But something nagged at the perimeters of her mind, something that didn't add up.

But it was forgotten when he said huskily, 'I'll have to take those stockings off,' and slid warm firm hands beneath her skirts, dealing with tricky suspenders, touching the heated satin of her inner thigh, making her heart lurch.

The wisps of torn silk discarded, he began to bathe her feet, dabbing ointment on the cuts and grazes after drying them gently with the towel he'd brought.

Then, wordlessly, he picked her up, carrying her upstairs, and she succumbed to the temptation to curl her arms around his neck, to rest her flushed cheek against the solid wall of his chest, hearing his heart beat in a restless tattoo that precisely echoed her own.

'Did you mean what you said about loving me?' he questioned as he laid her down carefully on the quilt that covered the huge bed. Hesitantly her eyes sought his but he was avoiding her gaze, and she put the hoarseness of his voice down to the exertion of carrying her upstairs. 'When did you know you loved me?' he persisted, almost tersely, as if it really mattered, going to flick on a bedside light, standing behind it so that she couldn't read his expression.

Hoisting herself into a sitting position, she knuckled her eyes. He certainly intended getting his pound of flesh, and she said, her voice muted, 'Quite early on—the day you ordered me to accompany you to dinner with Philippe Recaud and Fleur Moreau. I'd already discovered you had the guts and determination of ten,' she confessed, 'that you cared about your fellow human beings, cared enough to do positive good. And I'd known, almost from first setting eyes on you, that you were the most physically exciting and stimulating man I'd ever met—or was ever likely to.' She was about to add that her jealousy at seeing him in Cannes with Fleur had finally shocked her into admitting her feelings to herself.

But he cut in, 'Why didn't you tell me then?' He had moved closer, silently, but she could feel his presence near her, the raw sexuality she was so attuned to, and she raised her eyes to meet his at last and recognised a look of warmth. Of more than warmth?

'It knocked me sideways,' she said huskily. 'I'd been falling in love with you without realising it. While we were travelling Europe there were times when I almost told you—we seemed to be growing so close. But when we got home you changed, you were so distant. Besides,' she tagged on with a stubborn lift of her chin, 'I didn't know how you'd feel about it. My falling in love with you might have messed up our "arrangement". You didn't love me, and——'

'Didn't love you!' He was on the bed with her, dragging her into his arms, into the curve of his body. 'I think I fell in love with you the first time I saw you, at Ascot. Like you, my darling, I didn't know what had hit me at first. I thought it was mere lust—added to a rather selfish need to humble you! When we were introduced you aimed a frosty little smile over my left shoulder and then looked straight through me. I felt an immediate, overwhelming need to take you in my arms and kiss that haughty look off your face!'

'I don't even remember the occasion properly. I had the mother and father of all migraines,' she mumbled against his shoulder, feeling her heart soar, her brain grow dizzy, because he had said the incredible. He loved her!

'So that was it?' She heard his amusement through the wall of his chest, and then he told her, 'Where I grew up beauty was unknown. We were surrounded by dirt, slums and squalor. So I grew up with an appetite for beautiful things. When I got to London I haunted art galleries, parks, simply looking at beautiful things. I had a hunger for beauty in any form. I couldn't appease it.'

He began to stroke her bright hair, twining his fingers in the glossy strands. 'In a strange way, that hunger was both sharpened and appeased when I saw you. You were, quite simply, the most beautiful thing I had ever seen. A work of art come to life, a poem translated to flesh and blood, a song of perfection. I remember what you were wearing, the way you spoke, the way you walked. Everything. And you looked straight through me, as if I wasn't fit to sully the ground you walked on, and I knew then that I had to possess you. You were in my blood, a sweet poison, a dark magic, a mystery. You were all those things and more.'

He held her head into the curve of his neck and she wriggled closer, wondering how one human body could contain so much joy. She pressed her warm lips to his skin, tasting him, and he said thickly, 'You haunted my soul, my darling, you made my heart sing. You put me in the prison of your enchantment and threw away the key.'

The beauty of truth was in his voice, the raw edge of deep emotion slicing through to her heart, making tears well in her eyes, and she said thickly, 'I meant all that to you, and you didn't tell me!'

'How could I?' He kissed the tears from her face, raising himself on one elbow, love looking out of his eyes. 'From the way you'd reacted when we were introduced, I'd gathered that you couldn't even bring yourself to speak to someone like me. Shush——' He silenced her hot denials with his lips, then grinned down at her flushed face. 'I guess I was wrong about that, but I did my homework and found that you came from a fairly exalted background, that you hobnobbed with the cream of county society. I tried to imagine what you would say if I tried to date you—and didn't like the answer I gave

myself. I didn't come out of the top drawer in the stand—
I was firmly down there with the fluff underneath it!
Now, while that didn't bother me, I imagined it would
bother you, and I was working on a way to overcome
your scruples when I had to go to the States. When I
got back, I went—as you know—to Lassiter's, looking
for Pierre. I found your father. I'd already cultivated
his acquaintance, with a view to getting to you, and had
discovered his shaky financial situation. And luck
smiled.' He traced the outline of her mouth with a lazy
finger. 'No, dammit, she actually laughed out loud! I
was handed the means of possessing you on a plate! The
rest you know.'

'But I don't,' she denied, winding her arms around
his neck as his mouth very effectively silenced her words.
And later, though aching with the need he induced, she
managed, 'Why didn't you tell me how you felt, later?'

'My body told you,' he said thickly. 'That was as much
as I dared risk. And don't forget, I still thought you
were in love with Howard.'

'And I thought you just liked to have a willing female
in your bed, and if Fleur wasn't available, I would
do——' She broke off, gasping, as his hand gentled her
aroused breast. 'And in any case,' the words were
breathy, difficult to articulate, 'you'd told me you only
wanted to marry me because of some stupid need to be
accepted by the county set.'

'County set?' he grunted, finding her earlobe, nib-
bling, sending ecstatic shivers down her spine. 'I'm not
remotely interested in belonging to anything so outdated
and boring. I'm my own man, Ross Donahue. I don't
need such trappings; to belong to any clique.'

'But you said——'

'I know what I said,' he responded, a chuckle breaking through his voice. 'I couldn't tell you the truth—that I'd been going crazy over you ever since I'd first seen you—so I came up with the sort of guff I thought the type of woman I wrongly believed you to be would swallow.'

Lingeringly, he began to undo the row of buttons at the back of her dress. Her mouth moved to cover his, kissing him slowly, savouring him, heat growing inside her, her love for this man growing stronger because the growth of love never ends, and she said breathlessly, 'The only sense we make is this. Love me, Ross. Never leave me,' and he slowly stripped the last scrap of clothing from her body and lowered his head to her throbbing breasts.

'I'll love you forever, my darling, to forever and back again,' and then, in the soft darkness of night, the talking was over and the journey to heaven began.

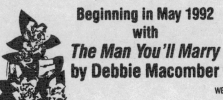

Following the success of WITH THIS RING, Harlequin cordially invites you to enjoy the romance of the wedding season with

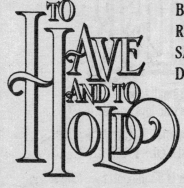

BARBARA BRETTON
RITA CLAY ESTRADA
SANDRA JAMES
DEBBIE MACOMBER

A collection of romantic stories that celebrate the joy, excitement, and mishaps of planning that special day by these four award-winning Harlequin authors.

Available in April at your favorite Harlequin retail outlets.

THTH

HARLEQUIN PROUDLY PRESENTS A
DAZZLING CONCEPT IN ROMANCE FICTION

One small town,
twelve terrific love stories.

TYLER—GREAT READING…GREAT SAVINGS… AND A FABULOUS FREE GIFT

Each book set in Tyler is a self-contained love story; together, the twelve novels stitch the fabric of the community.

By collecting proofs-of-purchase found in each Tyler book, you can receive a fabulous gift, ABSOLUTELY FREE! And use our special Tyler coupons to save on your next Tyler book purchase.

Join us for the third Tyler book, WISCONSIN WEDDING by Carla Neggers, available in May.

Janet Dailey's perennially popular Americana series
continues with more exciting states!

Don't miss this romantic tour of America through
fifty favorite Harlequin Presents novels, each one set
in a different state, and researched by Janet and her
husband, Bill.

A journey of a lifetime in one cherished collection.

May titles **#31 NEW MEXICO**
  Land of Enchantment

  #33 NEW YORK
  Beware of the Stranger

◈ *Harlequin*®

JANELLE TAYLOR

Valley of *Fire*

HARLEQUIN IS PROUD TO PRESENT *VALLEY OF FIRE* BY JANELLE TAYLOR—AUTHOR OF TWENTY-TWO BOOKS, INCLUDING SIX *NEW YORK TIMES* BESTSELLERS

VALLEY OF FIRE—the warm and passionate story of Kathy Alexander, a famous romance author, and Steven Winngate, entrepreneur and owner of the magazine that intended to expose the real Kathy "Brandy" Alexander to her fans.

Don't miss VALLEY OF FIRE, available in May.

Available at your favorite retail outlet in May, or reserve your copy for April shipping by sending your name, address, zip or postal code, along with a check or money order for $3.99 (please do not send cash), plus 75¢ postage and handling ($1.00 in Canada) for each book ordered, payable to Harlequin Reader Service to:

In the U.S.

3010 Walden Avenue
P.O. Box 1325
Buffalo, NY 14269-1325

In Canada

P.O. Box 609
Fort Erie, Ontario
L2A 5X3

Please specify book title with your order.

Canadian residents add applicable federal and provincial taxes.

TAY